*f*ive island diaries:
stories of love, lost and found

Spartan
Press

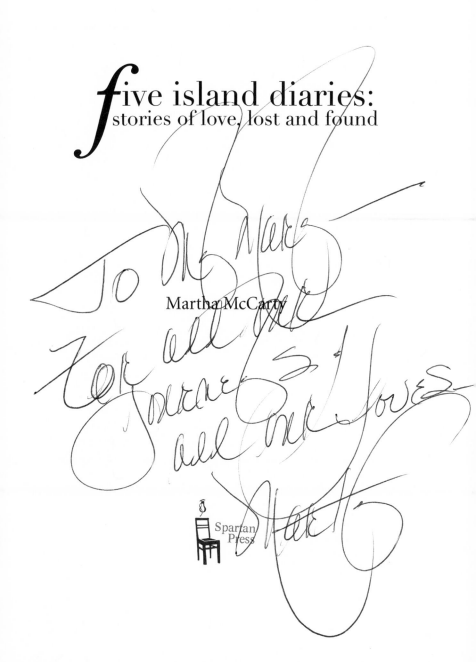

*f*ive island diaries:
stories of love, lost and found

Martha McCarty

Spartan
Press

Spartan
Press

1800 West 39th Street
Kansas City, Missouri 64111

Copyright © 2007
by Martha McCarty
ISBN: 0-9729114-9-9
Library of Congress Control Number: 2007902756

First Edition
1 3 5 7 9 10 8 6 4 2

Cover Design: Tim Blumer
Design & Layout: Tim Blumer & Spartan Press

Events described in these stories are drawn from actual circumstances. Some characters are composites and some names and
characteristics have been modified or changed. The author is solely
responsible for the content.

A Prospero's Bookstore selection
www.prosperosbookstore.com
www.fiveislanddiaries.com

for R. Kent *and* Jeffrey
my precious sons, my true believers

five island diaries: a foreword

Rain fell in the morning. In the afternoon, sleet and finally, snow. I watched from the window until Barb, my sister, called.

"I've been thinking," she said, crossing the miles by telephone. "You can write for others from now until forever, but it's time you write your own story. Just be honest," she said. "Tell the truth."

Truth, I answered, is an apparition. It comes and goes. I see it when others don't. Sometimes I run from it. Other times, I pursue. I examine it, analyze, question and surmise. But to capture truth, to print it on a page, called for insight and courage that was greater than mine. So one winter passed, then another. New snows came down like blurry curtains. Now near the close of a day, I look into the haze and I try to lay truth to rest, to lull it to sleep in the bed of a book by the sound of my voice, one word strung to another like tiny islands, awash in the only reality I know.

five island diaries: acknowledgements

The journey from what a writer knows to what must be learned is long and uncertain; that's why I am grateful for the chorus of cheerleaders whose sustained hurrahs along the way kept me writing, pushing on without a promise of ever finding a publisher, connecting with a reader, or earning a dime.

First on board were characters, inhabitants of my mind who had their own stories to be told. Then Beth Morrison read early scenes from *five island diaries*. Kindly, she said *write more.* Forty-one thousand words and bushels of crumpled up drafts later, *five islands* is in print—thanks to poet and publisher, Will Leathem who lovingly took the title in as if it were a foundling on the steps of Spartan Press.

For the encouragement of my sons and family, the

McCarty clan, I am more than grateful; I am rich. Thank you also to an ever-patient audience—Linda Wiedmaier, Melissa Anderson, Frank Polleck, Geoff Smith, Laura Muir and George and Eileen Lockwood—who listened as I repeated tales from *five islands* endlessly as stories formed in my head.

I am thankful, too, for a rare collection of friends, colleagues and fellow writers: Dee Zvolanek, Sharon Chapman, Mark Mustain, Dr. Ellen Spake, Mary Rose, Julia Ergovich, Marc Robinson, Lauren Miller, Dr. Lynn Casey and Father Bob Mahoney (he who writes like Nabokov).

Editor Cheeni Rao and noted author and mentor, Whitney Terrell, earn special praise for issuing compassionate critiques and unrelenting expectations, the compass points every writer needs.

five island diaries

Contents

The past is the present, isn't it? It's the future, too.
-Eugene O'Neill,
Long Day's Journey Into Night

Touched by the Fire

The summer my brother burned was a lonely one. Doc Moore, the nearest neighbor, ran out of his house and rolled my brother in a patch of grass near the weeping willow tree to put out the fire. Doc bundled the little boy's body into his arms and carried it to the ambulance. My brother's football helmet was still on his head, his scrimmage shirt stuffed with shoulder pads still on his back. Number eight. Same as his age. The rest of us, Mom, Dad, the neighbors, my big brother, my sister and Bobby, the boy who set my brother on fire with a lighted match and lawnmower gas, stood by the drive, stunned as Doc carried him away, skin dripping like candle wax from the bones of a little boy's legs.

It was the summer I turned ten, the summer I was more grown up than I wanted to be. Years after, memories of the fire unexpectedly ignited in my mind and I felt the flash of terror. I saw myself stiffened, gazing out on the backyard through the frame of the kitchen window, assaulted by screams, my brother ablaze, whirling in flames that licked his legs from the bottom up, covering his limbs like burning leaves. Then hysteria.

Mom, Dad, and Dickie, my big brother, followed Doc to the hospital. Barb and I were shepherded next door in the care of Doc's wife, Lillian. An R.N. before she had married, Lillian comforted my sister and me as if she were on night watch and we were ailing patients. She tucked her legs under her torso and burrowed into the sofa pillows, cradling us in her softness. She stroked my head, parting streams of hair with her finger tips, imploring me to be brave, to say a prayer, to let Doc take care of things.

"Your brother's in good hands," Lillian said. "Doc's and God's."

The din in my brain quieted as I gave in to Lillian's lap, hushed momentarily, eyes tight, feeling I might suffocate from fear, from the fright of the unknown, thoughts of the fire lost to other images. I remembered a small fish I had found stranded in sand as I scuffed along the lake shore one sunny afternoon. I studied the fish that had washed ashore, fascinated by the sad, desperate pulse of its gills flapping open, then shut, as it begged for air. Its eye pleaded with me as it fanned blue-white fins on baked sand and struggled to live. I stared at the fish for a long time and, not wanting to touch it, flipped it over with the toe of my sandal, shocked that its other fish eye stared at me, too. I thought it too sick to swim so, in uncertainty, I wandered away and left the fish to slowly suffocate, its silver body glistening in the sun.

Lillian continued to stroke, her hand on my hair, her voice a purr, her skin the scent of Ivory, but I was unconsoled. I had tumbled that night into faithlessness, an unforgiving witness to life's impermanence. I understood the desperation the little fish had telegraphed. I wanted to cry, but terror damned my tears. My eyes felt wide and dry like the fish eyes. My chest clenched and I thought my heart might stop I was so afraid—not that my brother would die (I couldn't comprehend that) but that I would feel the heat of my mother's tears as if they had fallen on me. As if I had somehow caused them. As if

I fulfilled Sister Rega's prophetic warning that children, born as innocents, choose to travel unholy trails, their sins mounting until God has no choice but to punish. How could I know what sins I had committed that had made God so furious, that had made my brother burn and my mother sick with tears? I felt I would never breathe again and there was nothing Lillian or anyone could do.

By midnight, my brother had returned, delivered home on a gurney, expected to die among family on a bed set up in the living room. He screamed in his dreams and fought to live, like the fish on the sand. Mom kept a vigil at his bedside. I hid in my upstairs bedroom, door closed, trying to blind myself to the hospital bed and the sheets that concealed his burns. Father Farrelly, robed in his long, black cossack, swept through the front door to administer Extreme Unction, the last sacrament. I tiptoed down the stairs in stocking feet and watched, hidden in the shadows of the hallway. Father lit blunt, white candles that were round and thick as his fingers. He ignited one wick with a match and transferred the flame to the second candle by touching it with the first. Reciting a prayer in Latin, he hovered, unwrapping my brother's hands and feet and swabbing them with cotton.

"In Nomine Patris," he prayed, making the sign of the cross and touching a crucifix to his lips, ministering as if the bed had become an altar.

"Holy Father, physician of souls and of bodies..." Father whispered, "heal Thy Child, Jerald McCarty, from the bodily infirmity that grips him, and make him live through the grace of God."

Heads bent, the family, all except me, knelt. Father blessed his patient with holy oils though their perfumes failed to mask the smells of burned skin, blood, and ointment that oozed through the bandages. In the hours after Father's ritual, my brother showed signs of strength, giving Doc the impetus to negotiate a room in the burn center at University Hospital. Arrangements were made. Mom would ride in the back of the ambulance to caress her son's hands, kiss his forehead, and ease him over bumps in the road on the three-hundred mile trip. Dad would work, then drive to Iowa City, leaving before dark on Friday nights, coming home on Sundays. Barb and Dickie would stay by themselves; they were old enough, Dad said.

I was whisked away to the farm.

Road to Wellness

"You'll be fine," Mom promised. "We'll come home. Soon as we can. As soon as your brother gets better."

She tucked a note into my shirt pocket, then slid behind the steering wheel and pointed our Chevy Fleetline toward town, leaving me, rubber sheet tucked under my arm, standing in gravel at the tip of a country lane, pretending my visit was a vacation. I watched Mom wave through a spot of sun that splashed on the car window and I thought *my mom is pretty* as the Chevy disappeared in the distance, clouds of dust devouring her. I stared at the highway, hoping to see her coming back to get me, but other than a frog-green John Deere lurching toward a cornfield, the road was empty. I saw no cars except Grandpa's old Ford parked by the barn. I imagined climbing into it, driving myself home, amazing everyone.

"Let's take your suitcase in the house and get out of the sun. Summer days make me sleepy," Grandma said, slowing me to the tempo of the farm.

Inside, the oven had made the kitchen hot but a breeze trickled through the window and mingled with the smell of applesauce and spices bubbling on the stove. Grandma stuffed me with oatmeal cookies, warm ones with raisins, then invited me to lay down beside her for a nap, my stomach plump with milk and sugar. She slept. I laid awake, watching lace curtains flutter in the window, feeling the east breeze stream across the bed and play on my face. Sleepless, I left the bed where Grandma snored, her teeth soaking in a water glass on the night stand, little bubbles floating around them. Beside her, as light and imperceptible as a paw print in the snow, the impression of my body on top of the quilt showed I had been there, pretending to sleep. Seated at her vanity table, a shelf stuck into a cubbyhole, I played with Grandma's powder puffs, colored my cheeks with contents of her rouge pot, clipped clusters of rhinestones to my ears and tilted her church hats—my favorite, a big-brim stuck with pheasant feathers—over my right eye in the style of a movie star.

Bored by the stretch of idleness, I escaped outdoors in search of adventure. I picked up Grandpa's trail in the barnyard as he chased chickens for supper, setting off squawks that scattered the brood like marbles in dirt. He targeted two young hens whose instincts failed to warn them of impending danger from an ax-wielding farmer dressed in a straw hat and Oshkosh overalls. Grandpa lunged and nabbed the spindles of their legs and hauled them, scaly feet first, scarlet combs scratching at the grass, out past the barn, beyond the corn crib and the tool shed, into the orchard to sudden death. I kept up, marching in Grandpa's procession as he limped along, leaning to the right, favoring the leg lamed in a tractor accident, winding along a path through rows of trees to a clearing. There, he centered a hen's head on a stump and anchored the other hen to the ground with the boot of his good foot. He raised the hatchet an arm's length above his head and with a single fluid swoop brought it down hard, splitting the chicken's neck with the sharp side of the blade. Her severed head flew. Her comb thudded in the mud. Her

9

body flopped. Wings pounded the ground as if there were hope. Hot blood spat at me, striking me below the knee, dribbling down my leg into the cold muck that sucked my toes. My stomach lurched, my hands popped up to my face, shoulders hunched. I listened to her screams.

"Phantom clucks," Grandpa said. "It takes a few minutes before she knows she's dead."

I gazed through the latticework of my fingers, witness to the Grand Guignol of the barnyard until the convulsions stopped and the hens' dismembered heads lay, finally silent among the cinnamon skins of rotten apples on a sunless orchard floor.

By dusk, the chickens crackled in a cast-iron pan. The flesh of their breasts, legs and thighs sizzled in hot lard over Grandma's wood-burning stove. I had helped Grandma pluck their feathers. She let me strike the matchstick and singe the down hidden beneath their wings. I raised their scrawny bird arms and burned the hairs, cringing at the smell as I watched the down curl and shrink in the flame, depositing black dots in the pimples of their skin. We dipped their body parts in egg batter, rolled their pieces in flour, and laid them in the frying pan. Fitting a lid on the pan for the chickens to simmer, Grandma waddled to the porch where fern fronds arched from a pedestal with the grace of backstage ballerinas bending at the barre, touching the tips of their fingers to the floor. Through the screen door, Grandma syncopated her yodel to the clang of a dinner bell dangling from a nail.

"Yodel-lay-heeeee-hoooo!" She summoned the men to supper. Clang. Clang. Clang.

Leaving fatigue in the fields, farm hands formed a crooked line like cattle coming in from pasture at twilight, ambling toward the house, supper, and the soft part of the day. Grandma poured sudsy water into a tin pan and set it on a wash stand on the porch. The hands splashed cracks on their faces, eroding the earth imbedded on their skin, cleaning themselves for supper.

We arranged ourselves around the wooden table, cueing the grandfather clock in the corner to bong and the cuckoo on the wall to call out. Six times. The absence of conversation among hired hands at mealtime imposed a solitude, allowing a faint sick feeling, loneliness, to creep into my stomach and across my skin. I longed to hear the jangle of the phone, the earpiece rattling in its cradle on the side of the big oak box mounted on the wall, Grandma talking into the mouthpiece attached to a cord, telling Central that she would take the call.

"It's your mom!" I wanted to hear her say. I studied the phone, as if through concentration, I could will it to ring. Instead, prayers filled the silence.

"Bless us, Oh Lord, for these thy gifts which we are about to receive..." Grandpa prayed, granting God a gratuity for the feast of Grandma's pies, cakes and crusty, homemade bread smeared with churned butter and chunks of plum jam. I landscaped the food on my plate, using a spoon to forge a hollow in a mound of mashed potatoes so the gravy formed a pool and, with my first forkful, poured over neighboring vegetables. Milk that Grandpa had pasteurized rimmed the jelly jar I drank from; cold foam stuck to my lips. Centered on a platter between two bowls, one heaped with carrots and one with green beans, lay the guillotined chickens, delicious, golden and crisp, juicy when I bit in. Across from me sat Steven, the youngest farm hand, eating uninhibitedly, smacking, wiping his mouth with a denim shirtsleeve.

Steven made me wiggle in my seat when he looked at me with icy eyes and I thought *when I grow up, I might marry him.*

I liked boys, though I elected not to tell, preferring to sacrifice my feelings rather than defend, nursing the fear that boys might not like me back and Barb would ridicule and embarrass me. Besides, the Sisters at St. Ellen's predicted my future as a nun. They said I had a calling and I surrendered, adopting the idea as if I had dreamed it up myself. I pictured my face framed by a nun's headdress and imagined swishing through school corridors, black garments flowing as I rewarded obedient children with holy cards, as the nuns did to me. I knew I was a Catholic in the way I knew I was a girl. I was born that way, the choice predetermined, drawn not from a multitude of options, but from a single belief, an invisible, though binding, reality.

Grandpa signaled the meal's end by mopping up gravy on his plate with a crust of bread. Politeness kept me from following, but tradition forgave him. Grandma served slices of fresh rhubarb pie and Grandpa poured cream into his coffee until it turned to caramel. He tipped his cup and splashed the brew onto his saucer, lifting it to his lips to slurp it like soup.

"That's how they did it in the Old Country," Grandma reminded me. The ritual fascinated though I was not allowed to dip, dunk, or slurp. Dad's rules followed me to the farm.

Supper done, Grandma sent me out to the well to bring in water for washing the dishes. I pumped the handle and watched the water pour, sweet and cold, until the bucket filled. I gripped the wire handle with two hands to haul it back to the house, stopping to set the bucket down and twiddle my fingers in the pond, unsettling the gold fish that had grown old and plump circling in the complacency of the cow's watering hole. I peered into the water as if expecting an image to take shape, as if I might dream Mom's face into existence through the ripples of the water. She would smile at me, her tears now dry, and I would know she was coming to take me home, to put everything back the way it was, to glue our fragmented family together like pieces of the silver hand mirror I had dropped and broken, its reconstructed face cracked, its shards of glass imperfect, but bonded, stuck into place.

I lifted the bucket of well water and lugged it into the kitchen. Grandma boiled it in a kettle on the stove and shot it with a squirt of Ivory, creating a bubble bath to soak the dirty dishes till they squeaked when she ran her finger over them. By then, Gold Medal Flour had snowcapped Grandma's body, powdering her mountains and the bulges that strained her corset, a spine-stiffening contraption that laced up the front and caressed big bosoms that had nursed my mother and five other farm kids. As if they were made of bread dough, Grandma's ankles poofed over the tops of her Selby Walkers, her work shoes. Toes peeped through mouse holes she had cut with a razor blade to relieve the bunions that throbbed without mercy when a storm brewed.

"Pull up a chair," she said. "You can help me." My place was at her side, standing on the chair, belly up to the sink, wiping dishes with a cloth cut from Grandpa's long-johns, stretching to stack the plates on a shelf in the cupboard high above my head. Over time, the shuffle of Grandma's shoes had worn a path, opening the linoleum and baring floorboards in a trail between the pantry and the stove. She hid coins in a coffee can in the cupboard and as many years as I had known her, I had watched Grandma add up her egg money like an allowance, counting her nickels, dimes and quarters, saving for new linoleum.

On the farm, evening sneaked into the house and, with it, sounds and smells, invisible companions. In a parlor small enough to fit into the kitchen four times over, Grandpa yanked tangled wires from a pack of batteries in the vest pocket of his overalls, disconnecting his hearing aid, accepting the blessing of silence. The bosom of his easy chair embraced him. He prepared his smoke, planting a row of Bond Street in a tissue laid across his hand, rolling the paper with his fingers and thumb, licking the edge, sealing it with spit. He struck a wooden match against the rough seam of his overalls, teetered the cigarette on his lower lip and lit the tobacco. Halos of smoke hovered. The scent, his evening incense, filled his small sanctuary. He chanted songs from the Old Country, his psalms, the creak of the rocker in accompaniment, a crucifix on the wall, his symbol, reflecting the faith that carried him through hard times when hail killed crops, prices plummeted, and the bank sent notice. The loan was due.

In the kitchen, her holy place, Grandma lifted the bib of her apron over an orb of white hair and hung it on a hook. Embers in the stove, dampered, died down; a dish towel, folded in squares over the back of a chair, absorbed the evening air; oilcloth on the table, brushed clean of crumbs, reeked of flavors that had spilled onto it. Grandma plucked rosary beads blessed by the Pope in Rome from a drawer cluttered with spools of thread, buttons, knitting needles and yarn and resumed her place at the table to mutter evening prayers.

My perch was on a Montgomery Ward catalog on the seat of a chair where I observed, my forearms, elbows, and chin resting on the table, eyes level, capturing a vision of the world as if photographically, images recorded, though it would take a lifetime for a clear picture to come into view.

Her eyes half open and half closed, Grandma rolled the rosary beads in the fat of her fingers, fondling them as she had night after night, year after year, washing away sins with prayers that flowed over beads until their shine was gone, offering her litanies to heaven, chanting streams of *Our Fathers* and *Hail Mary, Blessed Virgins.*

Stationed beside her, I felt myself drifting, voiceless and powerless, floating off, weighted only by a lonesome ache. The phone on the wall refusing to ring.

I awoke the next morning, dry. Beneath me lay crumpled evidence of a bedwetter's shame, the rubber sheet Mom had made me bring. Buoyed by the feather-bed in the upstairs bedroom, I had bobbed, adrift in goose-down pillows, toward morning. I hopped out of bed, a high one, and pressed my stomach to the floor, flattening my ear against the round hole that channeled heat upstairs in winter. The aroma of bacon, eggs, and potatoes browning in butter mixed with snatches of conversation and streamed through the opening. I listened, immobile and mute, hoping to hear clues to the future, sensing that truth had been withheld from me, believing Grandma and Grandpa knew more than they told, my worries magnified in the unknown. If Mom never came back, I feared I would live on the farm forever and grow old like Grandpa and Grandma, tall like the corn, drawing strength from the soil.

"Did my mom call?" I asked as soon as I went downstairs.

"She will when she has something to tell," Grandma answered. "It's long distance. All the way from Iowa City."

Grandma had already costumed herself for her role in the kitchen, her apron styled from flour sacks—scraps and rags she had stitched together by pumping the treadle on a Singer in a corner of the kitchen beneath a framed picture of Christ bleeding from a crown of thorns, his robes laid open to expose a wounded heart. I had watched Grandma sew before, fascinated with the rhythm as she pumped her right foot and hummed as she sewed, repeating patterns in a garden of yellow and blue bouquets, trimming her aprons in colored rickrack to match the flowers of the design. Strips of cloth became ties embracing her waist, folding into a bow behind her back.

After breakfast, she demonstrated homemaking skills, teaching me to flute the edge of a pie crust with my fingers and puncture the crust with a fork to release steam. I kneaded a batch of bread dough with my knuckles and buried my nose in the pillow of dough to intoxicate myself with the smell of baker's yeast. Grandma handed me a plate of soft butter.

"Smear this around the top of the bread pan before we put the dough in," she tutored.

"Why?"

"So the bread won't rise too high and go over the edge. Who'd want to crawl up the side of something so slippery?" she asked, sprinkling morsels of practicality into the dialogue, basic as bread crumbs. It was there in the camaraderie between an old woman who was hard-of-hearing and a child searching for comfort in the cadence of kitchen conversation, I learned to shape stories, to wander through the gossamer of the mind, as Grandma did, to sort through remnants of the day, to pull golden threads, to stitch and weave. To find filaments, then embroider and crochet. For Grandma, stitching and knitting were fundamentals in the rhythm of the farm, an intricate clockwork that registered through the senses. When day faded, primary colors dimmed to pastel, like lights fading on stage, a hush falling over the auditorium, all things becoming part of the pageantry. Chickens roosted in the hen house and cows settled into hay mounds in the barn, their swollen udders relieved of milk, their low moans mellowing as an apricot sky seeped into night. The creek, a watercolor, came alive in shades of azure or green. Peonies burst in Grandma's garden, inviting ants to picnic on blossoms of crimson or white. A clod of soil in Palo Alto County, the richest in the world, was so black, it looked blue. A handful of earth crumbled like a muffin and smelled as pungent and sweet. Morning came when the rooster crowed and kitchen scents circulated. Fragrances marked the days: Mondays smelled of laundry soap and clean sheets fluttering on the clothesline; Tuesdays, baked bread, fourteen loaves to last the week. By Sunday, the house had bathed in the spicy and sweet colognes of rhubarb sauce, apple cider, peach pies, honey-glazed ham, and home-rendered pork roasts.

Still, there was no one to talk to. No news, except noon market reports on radio station KLGA, announcing the price of corn and beans. Grandpa listened as if the voice of God the Prophet had come into the kitchen. Back home, Barb was having fun swimming, I supposed, and I was entombed in the tedium of the farm, apart from the family. I turned my imaginings over in my mind, rotating seeds of uncertainty that were buried deep, little worries growing like sprouts in plowed ground.

"Is my brother gonna be okay," I asked Grandma one night after prayers.

"I think I'll let your mama answer that when she comes home," Grandma sidestepped. "All we can do is pray," she said, applying prayer, her all-purpose remedy as liberally as a dose of Watkins salve she had daubed on my poisoned mosquito bites. When she caught me scratching the welts, she lifted the lid on the salve's container, the tin frame for a picture of old Mr. Watkins, a graybeard who looked official as a doctor and promised more: natural ingredients to calm and purify; to heal cuts and burns; to relieve sore, irritated skin; to draw out slivers or soothe bee stings. Grandma would dip her finger in the Red Clover Salve, swirling it around like peanut butter, smearing a glob on my sores.

"You can count on the Watkins Man," she said. "Every four weeks. Real regular. Coming down from the Watkins Medical Company in Minnesota. Never mind the cold or heat."

He carries a black bag and goes farm to farm, door

to door, dispensing Red Liniment, salve, insecticide for body-crawling insects, like spiders or the mosquitoes that bit me, Grandma reported. To me, the salve smelled like a mud puddle and it was gray, not green like clover, but it replaced the sting of my sores with a pleasant tingle.

"Why don't you go outside for awhile before it gets too dark," Grandma suggested one night after she had doctored me. "I'll give you a Mason jar and you can catch some fireflies."

Fresh-mown grass tickled the bottoms of my bare feet as I crossed the lawn, meandering, chasing fireflies beyond Grandma's garden, past the peas, the beans, the tomato and sweet potato vines, down the hill toward the South 40 where the air smelled of sweet corn. There, I sprawled on my back, splay-legged on a bed of grass before the dew came, facing heaven, tuning in to a chorus of crickets as day succumbed to night. I studied the strangeness of constellations until, like a shepherd on watch, I knew the stars by heart. Somehow, a change had drifted over me. I felt its relief, like when cool air chases away the heat. The prospect of welcoming a visitor pleased me; it was as if I had a secret. Grandma could offer him a piece of pie and pour him a cup of coffee, I thought, and we'd sort through his black bag. Grandma had promised that if I stayed long enough, I would see the Watkins Man coming down the road. I liked the idea of meeting someone out of the ordinary, someone who trafficked in cures and brought things to believe in.

When We Were Three

Mom and Jerry came home from the burn unit before the first snowfall. Thanksgiving was four weeks away, but Mom roasted a turkey to celebrate, to fill the house for a homecoming and a sense that the family was harmonious and whole. The turkey in the oven sent its aroma through the rooms, upstairs and down. Irish linen, washed, starched and pressed, dressed the dining room table. Grandma McCarty's golden-edged china, a link to Dad's past before he became a working man, was lifted down from the tallest cupboard, one fragile piece at a time. Barb and I lit candles and arranged plates next to crystal stemware that hummed when I ran my finger around the rims.

Doc and Lillian joined the feast, as if part of the family; after dinner, Doc encouraged Jerry to walk again on legs as shaky as a yearling's.

"Jeeeesus Chriiist! Dirty sonovabitchs!" Jerry screamed, folding in agony when he tried to take a step. He swore like a stevedore when he first stood on atrophied limbs that had shriveled until they were barely thick as broomsticks.

"It's the rush of blood pulsing to nerve endings," Doc said. "It feels like millions of pin pricks. It'll pass."

Mom and Dad, one on each side of my brother, propped him up, steadying him like crutches by holding his underarms as he inched through the dining room.

"He has to say those words," Mom said, unapologetically. "It's the only way he can release the pain. Cover your ears if you don't like it."

A realization rippled through my mind. More than the season had changed, making the occasion seem sad, not happy. Feeling useless, I retreated from the drama in the dining room and wandered out to inventory the neighborhood. The Elm that stood too close to the driveway had suffered a new cut while I was away, I noticed. Drivers turning in or backing out haphazardly had carved a history of knicks in the bark through the years we lived on Harrison Street.

"Don't worry about that old Elm," Mom had said, dismissing concern. "That tree's as strong and sturdy as your Daddy. And he's been through the war. I don't like to see it get hit, either. But it'll heal. Nature has a way of taking care of things."

True. The Elm ritualistically announced new seasons and renewed a cycle of growth rooted in a previous century. She shed her gown of russet and gold in October and returned refreshed in the spring, leafy and green, bathed in a musky cologne, weathering change in dignified silence. The latest cut in her skin had sliced to the quick. I ran my finger around the raw opening in the hard bark, feeling bumps from a crisp, dry coating the Elm had weeped to shield her wound and hold the sap inside. The earth at her feet had hardened and browned in anticipation of winter. Other than that, the neighborhood seemed the same. Sheriff and Mrs. Miller lived in the stone house on the corner. A curved sidewalk led to their front door, giving the Miller house the look of the cottage Snow White found in the forest. Mrs. Miller liked to bake Krum Kake from a Norwegian recipe and deliver it to neighbors for the holidays, yoo-hooing her way in through the door. I imagined the aroma circulating in the chilled air, as if cakes were baking in Mrs. Miller's hearth at the moment, the scent floating out through the chimney. Thankfully, Doc and Lillian, my favorites, still lived next door. But Bobby was gone.

Bobby and his family had gathered their belongings and chased away like a summer squall, soon after the fire. I walked down the block and turned on State Street to see their rental house abandoned, its windows stripped, its grass matted and in the backyard, a pair of Levi's still pinned to the line, snapping in the wind. The screen door dangled from a torn hinge and a nest of leaves rearranged itself in a corner of the porch where bicycles had been.

I felt poised and alone in the neighborhood, as if at the edge of something strong, though unseen. An inner signal delivered an eerie awareness I had not known before, a feeling of certainty without being shown, led, or told. I felt I had sniffed the unknown, like an animal sensing a storm. Winter would come, I knew, and with it, changes in the family that would yield consequences, inevitable as impending snow. If wishing could have made it so, I would have closed my eyes and brought the past summer into being again, like when drifting into sleep, creating a happy dream. Back then, Bobby and I had spent Saturday mornings skating in a circle around the band box at Harrison Park, stopping at the Dairy Queen for root beer floats. Just the two of us. The day of our last skate, Mom had plopped me in a chair to cut my hair before she let me go. She wrapped a towel around my neck as a barber's cape in the makeshift beauty shop where she stunk up the kitchen giving her sisters Toni home permanents on Saturday nights.

"Stop wiggling or I'm going to cut your ear off," she threatened. "It's hard enough to do this when you sit still," she said, clipping dangerously close with her sewing scissors, steadying her hand against my forehead. Snip. Snip. I heard the scissors nibble.

"Your hair's so scraggly and you're so skinny, I think I'll turn you upside down and use you for a broom," she said.

She fringed my bangs into a pixie and I felt sure that, thin as a flower stem, I looked like Audrey Hepburn: naked ears, cropped bangs, gander neck and all.

"There. It's darling," Mom said. "You'll set a new style." She unwrapped me, freeing me from the chair, snapping the towel out the back door, releasing clippings to the breeze, turning snips into spangles in the sun.

"See how you look. Then sweep up the floor and you can go. You'd better not skate on Mrs. Finnegan's sidewalk. She thinks you kids are the ones who climbed her apple trees."

We *were* the ones. The day I got stranded in Mrs. Finnegan's orchard was the day I fell out of a fruit tree into preadolescent love. Other kids had leaped from the limbs and scurried into the leaves of lilac bushes when Mrs. Finnegan, shrouded in a black shawl, blew the police whistle she carried on a string around her neck. Her crooked arms cranked the air and she sputtered like Dad's old Evinrude, puttering toward her backyard orchard to nab green-apple thieves. She wobbled unevenly, as if bunions were potato spuds in her shoes, struggling to pick up speed before everyone escaped.

Bobby didn't run. He stood in defiance beneath the limb where I clung, afraid to let go. Mrs. Finnegan collared him under the branches, jerking him by the neck of his T-shirt, warning him that she'd call the authorities if she ever caught him again.

"You're stretchin' my shirt," he said. Then Mrs. Finnegan laid a sharp slap on one side of his face, branding his cheek with red lines, thin as whip lashes from a widow's wiry fingers. Bobby didn't flinch.

I straddled, embracing indecisiveness as well as the branch. For some reason, I thrilled to what I witnessed below my loft in the tree. I felt fearful yet giddy, engaged though suspended, central to the scene while absent from it. I knew that revealing myself was an option and though I considered it, fascination with the ground-level action outlasted the impulse to confess. I stayed hidden in my perch, watching and listening, barely breathing, delicately balanced between truth and deceit. I tightened my arms, locking myself to the limb, clinging to duplicity as Bobby took the blows.

"What's the matter? Cat got your tongue?" Mrs. Finnegan demanded. As if she had mussed his dress uniform, Bobby straightened his shirt and stared her down as she gave her spiny finger a final wag in his face, forcing him to empty the apples from his pockets and ordering him off her property. I hung on the limb, inconspicuous as a cloud, concealed by branches heavy with apples until Mrs. Finnegan victoriously withdrew. She gripped her long, gunny-sack skirt with one hand, held a railing with the other, and hobbled up the unpainted steps of the back porch. Sun shined through the fibers of her skirt and flashed a glimpse of an old woman's shriveled limbs, crooked as the tree's, before she disappeared into her house through the screen door. Then Bobby emerged from the foliage between the bushes. Lord of the Orchard, he came to claim me.

"Jump," he said. "It's not that far." I dropped to the ground with a thud, like one of the fat apples.

"Come on," Bobby said. He jerked his head toward an opening and pranced like a horse in the forest, drawing me toward a passage between the bushes. In the alley, Bobby's bike had been planted in the gravel, propped on its kick stand, primed for a quick getaway. He threw his leg over the bar and wiggled into position on the tricornered seat.

"Hop on," he ordered. I balanced on the back, hugging him like I'd hugged the tree, and Bobby pedaled me home on a rattle-fendered Schwinn, the breeze fingering my hair. He lifted his feet off the pedals, held them out like airplane wings, and we whizzed past the creamery and the Conoco, careening down the mountains of the VFW hill, the slopes of sledding champions in winter.

The day of our last skate, I waited for Bobby on a park bench down by the lake, the sun a spotlight on my fresh haircut. As a diversion, I ran my fingertip down drips of Park Department paint, thick as emerald ice cream, frozen in motion, caught on the run between slats on the back of the bench. I glanced at the bathhouse and, spotting him, I slipped my hand into the warm well of a side pocket in my camp shorts and fingered the skate key tied to a shoelace, initiating a game. I pulled the key from the pocket bottom and danced it before Bobby's face, knowing he would snatch it from the air, knowing he would kneel on the sidewalk before me, bony knee on bare cement, unflinching as if the stone were satin, knowing Kate O'Connor could see us through her bedroom window in the house across the street, knowing a boy liked me.

"I can't get my skates tightened by myself," I faked. "Gimme the key."

Kneeling, Bobby untangled the heap of hardware piled in the grass, the clamps, wheels and plates of my Sears and Roebuck skates. He squeezed my feet, first the left, then the right, guiding them into the metal molds, tightening the latches on the sides till they hugged the soles of my sandals. Except for the freckles splattered on his face, how Bobby looked is hazy in memory. I remember only a temptation to touch, to feel the curls on his head with the brush of my hand, reverently, like a princess with a peasant boy on his knees in adoration.

I knew Bobby's reputation. I knew he was weird. Wicked. Maybe dangerous. He had long fed our adventure-starved appetites for gossip in the day's debriefing at supper time. Tales of his antics passed around the table as if they were side dishes, tasty as heaps of mashed potatoes and gravy.

"Bobby drowned Mrs. Olsen's cat in the lake on the way home from school today," Jerry reported one night over a tuna casserole. I picked the peas out of my noodles, steered them to the side of my plate with the edge of a knife and listened, captivated by Bobby-stories.

"I saw him. Me 'n Brennan," Jerry said. "He bashed its head with a ball bat and held it under 'till it was croaked."

"Why didn't you stop him?" Dad asked. "You could've stopped him, couldn't you?"

On the playgrounds, Bobby was odd man out, least likely to be picked for the baseball team, most likely to be suspended from school. He was notorious at St. Ellen's where Father Farrelly had ousted him from altar boy class after he had torched a pile of cassocks with a vigil light and run. Once a week, Father's girth and the offense of his breath filled the room when he visited catechism classes, commanding attention from the front of the room, the strength of his halitosis reaching as far as the back row. Sister Rega, the oldest nun and the scrawniest, lined the front row with boys she snatched with one swoop to box their ears when she judged them to be rowdy. Always, Bobby occupied a front seat in direct line of Father.

"Good morning, Father," the class chimed when Father stepped through the door sharply at eight on Mondays to lead morning prayers and the Pledge of Allegiance.

All stood beside the desks.

"Good morning, boys and girls," he answered, predictably. "You may be seated."

Father was bigger than any man I had ever seen, including Sheriff Miller. He had been the Diocesan priest stationed in our parish, titular head of a small theocracy since the War when the men were gone. He had married Mom and Dad, baptized the four of us, and had given us our first communion. Whenever I saw Father, I was conscious of his clean fingernails and hands, his skin porous, bleached-white and speckled as bark on a birch tree. It was as if Father had never touched anything soiled, only the communion wafers he inserted into my mouth to melt on my tongue because chewing them was a sin. By the time Father was elevated to Monsignor, gray hair edged his ears and the balloon that was his face jiggled over the choke of his cleric's collar.

"Robert," he said to Bobby after the vestibule incident. The power of Father's voice was contained in its muffled rumble, a potential eruption ever present, the force of his authority shutting out competing sounds. Sister dinged the hotel bell on her desk three times to signal quiet and the room settled. Hands folded on desks, everyone listened, speaking only if invited.

"Stand up, Robert," Father said. "I'm afraid we have to make an example of you." He grabbed Bobby by the arm, yanking him out of the seat and jerking him into place in front of the room to demand a public confession so the stain of Bobby's wrong doings bled into our consciousness and the snickering of classmates lived beyond the occasion of sin.

"If you know someone who has done something wrong, like Robert here," Father said, patting Bobby's shoulder, making it appear that the two were com padres, that Father conferred on Bobby an honor, rather than humiliation.

"If you know someone who has committed a sin, told a lie or cheated on a test—stealing another's answers," he paused as if imagining such a serious offense for the first time, although the lesson had been laid out on a string of Monday mornings.

"What must you do?"

"Report it," the class said, all together. "Tell Sister!"

"Tell Sister!" Father repeated, the boom of his voice

authenticating our response. "Set a good example."

Setting an example, either good or bad, passed as Father's favorite trick in his holy bag of magic.

"Tell Sister," he said. "Then drop that person like a hot potato," he said, his voice dipping on the words *drop that person*, as if acknowledging a sad but necessary action.

"Drop that person like a hot potato," he repeated the instruction for reinforcement.

I imagined Father's eyes settling on me; I feared he had guessed my secret. My sense of guilt aroused, he might as well have pronounced my name; I, who had collected stacks of holy cards Sister Rega awarded for performing acts of good faith; I, who stopped just short of sainthood in Sister's estimation; I, a good reader and speller, the obedient one who had never confessed that I liked the boy Sister dubbed *the divil himsilf* with her lingering Irish brogue. Bobby had been branded, but when no one was looking, he had been gentle with me. I had discovered a quality unrecognized in Bobby as if I had found a scared kitten mewing, stranded in the back of the barn, a creature who needed somebody to be nice. In my mind, Bobby's evil had been redeemed, vanquished by the spell of kindness he had revealed to me.

Rejected and scorned in school, he pretended indifference. He had grown restless by fourth grade, begging for attention, indulging in the bizarre, transforming at times from The Tormented to The Tormentor. He held a stick over a bonfire and when it blazed orange-red, he rammed it into his dog's rectum, delighting in the animal misery, the yelping, hobbling, and tail chasing he caused. The scene comes to mind, eerily so, in reflection. Then, I heard no voices, not even my own. Only the dog's piercing whine can be detected. Smoke from a fire built of dry sticks and leaves tinged the atmosphere and through it, neighborhood kids surrounded flames like heathen children in the woods of Salem, entranced by a spectacle, tainted by denial. Thinking at first that the gathering was for fun, I soon knew that Bobby had crossed a boundary. His demons unchained, Bobby had hurt Tippy, his mongrel pup, spellbinding an audience. Excited by the horror, yet feeling sick, dual forces of conscience clashed in my mind and I stood motionless as the others, measuring right against wrong, balancing the desire to belong and the need to be true, comparing the benefit of silence against the cost of intervention, replacing honor with inaction. I nursed an impulse to let pass what Bobby had done. Indecision absorbed my voice like the smoke in my clothes. I stood in the crowd, soundless, as if carved from cardboard or pliable clay. I wanted someone to speak. To act. I didn't want it to be me, though I knew that complicity was no trivial sin. Through my mind's confusion, an instinct finally rang clear, its message subtle, yet distinct as the sound of a wind chime. If I chose to listen.

My reflex was to retreat. In a way, I did.

"Bobby!" I shrieked, piercing the silence, stamping my foot in indignation. I glared at Bobby centered in the circle near the fire, smoldering stick in his hand, a smirk on his face as if he expected applause.

"Why did you do that?" I pounced, wrangling the stick from his hands, using it to whop him on his back and his neck with a wrath equal to Carry Nation ripping into a saloon, blows powered by righteousness. Bobby hunched, shielding his face from the lashes, howling louder than Tippy had.

"I'm tellin'!" I announced. I turned, heel digging into

the dirt, breaching the bonds of the pack, legs wobbly and unreliable, dropping a hot potato as I ran for home.

"You ever see anything like that, you stop him. Or else," Dad said, lecturing Jerry.

"You girls better not play with Bobby anymore," Mom said, reinforcing a prevailing philosophy: boys are wiley enough to fend for themselves; girls are not. With that, she signaled the end of music lessons Bobby's mother had given me in her living room on an upright piano with ivory keys, three chipped, the piano back pressed against the living room wall beside the window. If I leaned to the left while seated on the bench, I took in a view of the yard where neighborhood kids played *Olley, Olley Olsen, All in Free* under an ancient Oak that leaned protectively, her roots sunken in soil like an elephant's foot. If the piano lessons ended, Mom might enroll me in Red Cross swimming lessons where, I worried, I would be forced to swim rather than float. Worse, Mom's decree aborted sidewalk skating with Bobby, one Saturday after another.

He and Jerry had stayed pals, playing ball in our yard and his. As consolation, Dad bought me a bicycle at the

Coast to Coast Store so I could ride to the lake or across town to Ginger's, my friend since kindergarten, except Ginger summered at Camp Foster on Lake Okoboji. I elected not to join her, hiding the fear that I might wet the bed in the camp bunkhouse. Excluded from the boys' club and friendless for the summer, I shined my bike, wheeling it into the backyard, spraying the maroon and pink-striped fenders with a garden hose at least once a week, no matter the weather. But I felt alone.

Barb didn't like me; she said I was prissy. I could spell and read out loud for story hour at the library, write poems and sew—nothing other kids liked to do. Deceitfully, I followed the boys on my bike one blistering afternoon, spying on them as they pedaled past homes, shops and stores that circled the shores of Five Island Lake. Ditching their bikes in the weeds, they climbed onto the Rock Island Bridge, a huge, steel span above the water. I, stationed in the shade of a Maple tree, watched them fish from on high, perched on the railroad trestle, their heads touching the treetops. They lured Bullheads and Northern Walleye with bite-size minnows shimmering at the end of the lines they dangled in the water, soon inventing their own style of fishing: tossing poles, clamping thumbs and forefingers to their noses and, skinny arms spinning like pinwheels, plunging into the water at will, crawling back up through weeds, grins on their faces.

I decided to go home and scrub my bike again in the backyard. Unpopular and alone, I left the boys and the games I wanted to play. There they would stay, loving a close call, dangling on the edge of the railroad trestle until the track shimmied and a distant whistle warned that danger thundered their way.

In the Game

Dad honked the horn, three toots to get attention when he pulled in the drive after working his holiday shift at the light plant. Memorial Day weekend, the summer of 1954, the sunlight a cool stream, not yet hot, though the ice had gone out of the lake in April. He slammed the driver's side door and in a step that imitated a skip, scurried to the rear of the Ford Fairlane he had financed on time payments, a sign that the wages of war had been written off to the previous decade.

The Ford was two-tone blue, light against dark. Its roomy insides smelled like new shoes. A chrome strip zipped along side panels, linking headlights to taillights and a trunk that was big enough to hide a surprise. Dad jammed the key into the lock, popped the trunk, and rooted through the cavern as if it were a back closet, extracting its prize: a red leather bag, saddle-stitched in white, stuffed like a Christmas stocking with trinkets.

The bag held a set of golf clubs. The putter clanked against irons and produced a tinny-sounding song as Dad hauled his bounty into the house, parading through the kitchen to the dining room. He propped the bag against a wall and stood back.

"They're Sam Snead's," Dad announced. The family circled, as if viewing a lamp with the magic of Aladdin inside.

"A full set of Signature Sam Snead's," he said. "Ray willed them to me when he died.

"These are the best clubs ever made," Dad said, his voice altered by a hint of reverence, his quiet tone forcing attention though Dad's inspiration, I thought, was not Ray, a dead man, but Sam Snead, a golfer.

He grabbed the strap and looped it over Jerry's shoulder, tilting him with the weight of the clubs. The shafts had been shined, the clubs scrubbed clean, the woods waxed to a gloss that caught light beams, a shining reflection of Ray's last act.

"They're yours," Dad said, the respectful quality adding credence to his words.

"If...," he paused.

Curiosity kicked in and the impulse to ask, "If what?" flooded the moment. But nobody stirred; this was Dad's magic act, the family a rapt audience.

"If...," he said, stretching the question. "If you go out to the golf course and play. Every day. Get out and build your muscles," Dad said, striking a bargain with my brother. "Get your strength back."

Hobbled by his injury, Jerry had stayed out of school after the fire, missing third grade, withdrawing behind walls, fitting pieces into a jigsaw puzzle set up on a card table, staring out windows at a colorless, cold-shouldered geography. Winter had been her usual severe and uncharitable self that year, withholding warmth as if intending to punish, blinding drivers in blizzards of snow, sealing the lake in a cake of ice, suffocating Silver Bass and schools of Great Northern Pike, depriving the water of oxygen. Short on news, the *Emmetsburg Reporter* ran bowling and basketball scores alongside reports of fourteen-inch snowfalls and thirty-seven endless days of sub-zero temperatures, registering no sign of an early thaw.

The March of Dimes Poster Girl shivered in minus nine-degrees, struggling down Broadway on crutches and leg braces, earning donations at ten cents a step for the polio drive. All grades at St. Ellen's collected dimes to aid the cause of victims entombed in iron lungs, their limbs frozen, hair and faces protruding from the metal tubes, as if only heads, not bodies, might be salvaged. Nuns clipped Kodachrome pictures from *Life* magazine and taped them to the blackboard, scaring students into acts of charity, though no one at St. Ellen's had been stricken.

Home from the exile of the farm, I had resettled at St. Ellen's, appearing after school had started, satisfying Sister Domatilla, the Mother Superior, by scoring high on a review of fractions and language. She readmitted me to a cluster of fifth-grade classmates, Ginger included. As a celebration, Sister escorted me to the eighth-grade room to read holy stories out loud and to herald the return of her prodigy, a fluent reader, a bright, shiny penny in a nun's impoverishment. Climbing two flights of stairs, Sister at my side, the steps squeaked as the shuffle of our shoes—Sister's Selby Walkers; my Buster Browns (new, not hand-me-downs)—followed the hollows of wood sanded down by footsteps that had gone before, like those of my father's; his father's, too. I felt as I ascended that I had been called to an ancient tower, drawn into a chamber of giants where bold girls wore lipstick to school and hulking farm boys, if aggravated, could crush me. The room's hugeness made me feel shrunken in size, small as a six-year-old, and as if they had perched on a rooftop, the eighth-graders stared down from their elevation, wooden desks that were higher than my head. I started to feel that I needed to throw up, like when I swallowed an oyster on a dare. I knew if I vomited, Sister would send for Vincent, the school janitor, and Vincent would scatter a bucket of ashes on the mess before scooping it up with a shovel, leaving the room to smell long afterward. If I vomited, I worried, humiliation would be mine, so I squeezed my stomach muscles, forcing a showdown with fear. I studied my feet until I felt my legs stiffen like peg legs, securing my resolve. Encouraged by Sister's belief that I was special, extraordinary in a way, I fell in behind her nun's skirts and followed her to the front of the room, ignoring the eyes of the giants. There, Sister announced me by name and I stood as she had taught me: straight as a music stand. Opening the scriptures, I held the book high, its spine nesting in the palm of my left hand, the fingers of my right hand free to turn pages with the deftness of an accompanist sweeping through sheet music, mid-song. Sister stationed herself on the sideline, beaming. She cherished good spellers and readers, loving them more, I suspected, than she loved The Almighty.

My tongue rippling over the sounds, I read aloud, syllable by syllable, calmed by the power of spoken words.

Convinced that I was smarter than others at school, at home I was equally convinced of my insignificance. The household had become a harbor for worry; fear's presence, though invisible, darkened the nights, sneaking in while Mom focused on my brother's rehabilitation and Dad fixed on unworkable calculations. He had developed a tendency to scribble numbers and dollar signs on paper napkins after supper, computing hospital bills that had stacked up, unpaid.

"I make as much as any man in town and it's never enough," he complained. He waded through his computations, constantly it seemed, shaking his head like a dog chewing a rag, crossing out the totals, negatives.

"From now on, we're turning down the furnace. Sixty-degrees is enough when you sleep," he grumbled. "And I want you kids to turn off the lights every time you leave a room," he said, his words shot with the implication that children were the cause of his hardship. Without kids, Dad might have been as he appeared in old photos, a silk-suited figure, showcased against the grill of a Buick roadster, hair slicked back and parted in the middle. Instead, a cloud of silence, broken only by muffled outbreaks, followed him home and drenched the house in apprehension. If Dad felt helpless, shouldn't we all?

His child, I chose silence, too. I taught myself a trick to escape the bewildering world of our house. I learned to hold my mind still, barricading worry, crouching in Mom and Dad's bedroom closet, comforting myself with semiconsciousness, shadows engulfing me like heat from a register. Skipping homework one evening, I scrambled into my favorite place, hiding mite-like in the closet, quiet and shy. The game going on in my mind was one of wonder—how long would it take Mom to miss me? I knew they, the family, were out there; the sound of conversation seeped in through a crack in the door, like distant voices heard through a lifted window, near yet far. I could have sung a Rosemary Clooney song, but my voice would have signaled my whereabouts and I preferred concealment beneath the clothes, though I longed to be discovered.

Pieces of history hid with me in the closet, creating an odd eulogy to times I had never known. The scent of Mom's perfume lingering in the green silk dress she wore in the days when Dad had taken her to dances mixed with the sour smell of boots and shoes, leather and sweat. The hem of her dress felt cool and slick, like cold cream, when pressed against my face. In the back of the closet, a zippered bag leaked the odor of mothballs that preserved Dad's Army uniform, a pair of wool pants and an Eisenhower jacket, medals pinned to the chest, corporal's stripes stitched like bright welts to the sleeve.

Beneath a stack of hats on the highest shelf, a small wooden box rested, its lid sealed on Dad's military past. I had once been led to its secrets, an accomplice to Dickie, the only one who was brave enough to enter the dark of the closet and lift the lid. Barb and I joined an exhumation of its contents: a gold ring, cut from the finger of a dead soldier who never returned, we reasoned; a flag we unfolded and folded again by repeating each crease; a love letter from our mother; Dad's dog tags, and buried in the bottom, wrapped in an Army-issue handkerchief, a German Luger. A black and white Kodak snapshot, its glaze cracked by time, captured the image of a skinny boy standing near a tank, a desecrated village in the background.

"We still hear the sound of snipers in the hills," the inscription on the back of the photo said in Dad's handwriting, a dispatch from the past. By unsealing the box Dad had hidden in the dark as if his souvenirs and the War itself did not exist, we had unearthed his memories, clues to an unknowable man. Dad had guarded the privacy of war, though he often repeated a caution: "You kids better learn how to get along. Someday, it's gonna be up to you to keep peace in this world."

My absence from the family circle, finally, was noticed. Mom switched on the bedroom light and rousted me from my outpost. "Come on!" Mom said, opening the closet door, the light shocking to my eyes. "Get out here and rejoin the human race."

I crawled out of my cubbyhole on hands and knees, my eyes adjusting to reality, like when squinting in the sun after a movie matinee, exchanging the dark for daylight.

"I need you," Mom said. *I need you.*

"I need you to help with your brother's new therapy. If he doesn't do it, his legs could lock up," she said. "Freeze forever."

She didn't expound, but I felt a flicker, a moment of incandescence, an understanding that leaped like a flame from her mind to mine. She knew that hiding behind the heart is impossible because feelings, like my mom, seek and find. Besides, who wouldn't want to be discovered? In the space of a second, loneliness over, I left the stale satisfaction of retreat and swapped it for action.

Enlisted to aid in Jerry's therapy, a sense of importance joined me at the foot of my brother's bed where I stood. Needed. Comforted by the feeling that I was not separate but, in a way, one.

My brother stretched his body out vertically on top of the quilt, face to the ceiling.

"Warm up a little," Mom instructed. "Wiggle your toes till they feel real limber. Kinda tingly."

I bent like a volunteer charged with building a dike, lugging burlap sandbags from the floor, hoisting them with two hands, boosting the weights onto the bed.

"Put two bags on each foot," Mom said. I loaded the bags on my brother's toes.

"Okay," Mom directed. "Lift!" she said. "Right foot first."

One leg raised, barely an inch off the bed.

"We'll keep count," Mom said, forcing Jerry to use jellied muscles.

"One!" She counted.

A long time passed before Mom could say two, my brother's legs hardly moving beneath the sandbags.

"Two!" She finally announced.

On "three," I joined in, counting repetitions until, in weeks that followed, the leg lifts climbed to twenty, then thirty and more. One at a time. Three sessions a day. It was in that way that a quasi-friendship formed between my brother and me, friends by default, bonded by circumstance, time adding up like the measure of his exercises. Then came summer and Dad carted the Sam Snead's into the dining room.

"Bring the clubs," Dad had said, leading the family to the backyard. There in patches of grass, he taught the proper grip, fingers pointing down the shaft of a golf club, one thumb locking another.

"Play early in the morning before the course gets crowded," he said, laying down the rules. "Mom will drop you off and pick you up. When you're strong enough, you can ride your bike."

My brother nodded.

"Be polite when you're out there," Dad continued.

Jerry hit a whiffle ball across the yard and followed it through the grass. I had begun to lose interest, grateful that Dad didn't expect me to play golf.

"Replace divots," he said. "Don't throw your clubs when you hit a bad shot—and don't cheat on your score."

Jerry returned the ball and dropped it at Dad's feet, like Cookie, our cocker spaniel, bringing home a bone.

"Never, ever swear," Dad said. "Don't let me catch you losing your temper on the golf course."

The clubs might have been a collection of crutches

and canes, the way my brother learned to rely on them. From then until Labor Day, he committed to the game, playing daily, no matter the weather. Dad didn't join him; he abandoned my brother to his own resources, granting him the grace of self reliance, the strap on his bag of Sam Snead's biting into his shoulder.

At first, he played two holes, then a confident three, and four. Retirees who whiled away the hours at the golf course, old duffers, Dad called them, turned into mentors. The old men coached, teaching a lifetime of techniques to improve swing, putts, and scores. Seventy-five-year-olds who were more than sixty years his senior befriended my brother and, soon, Jerry traded my company for theirs. He napped in the locker room after a game and, vigorous by the end of summer, took up hunting golf balls to recycle and sell.

'You know how to make a sign?" he asked, inviting me to ride to the course with him one morning. "I need a sign that says: *Golf Balls - Good As New - 25 cents.*"

We rode our bicycles along the north shore, past the boat house, up a hill to the club. I tagged along as he scoured cornfields and ditches along the road, finding balls that had landed out of bounds. He rolled his pant legs to his knees and, while I lolly-gagged on shore, he waded in shallow water off Number Seven green, cupping his hands to drink fresh spring water that poured over boulders, bending to pluck balls out of muddy sludge.

"It feels like pudding squishin' between my toes," he hollered to me.

Mallards nested on Second Island, eating gnats and grass before leading their ducklings in a swim. The shoreline, a watery grave for balls sacrificed to the Par 5 dogleg, was to my brother, a nest of golden eggs. He scrubbed the rescued balls with a toothbrush. He shined, polished, recycled and sold balls by the bucket full—my cardboard sign taped to the door of the men's locker room as a marketing ploy. With a salesman's panache', he kissed the skin of a rejuvenated Spalding as he presented it with a loud smack to a customer.

"Look at this little beauty!" he said, before sacrificing a ball.

At dusk, we bicycled home, my brother still waterlogged and smelling like wood rot. I followed, pedaling fast, trying to keep up, wondering how to snag my share of the profits, the coins, dollar bills and five-spot that bulged my brother's pant pockets. The family as his gallery at supper time, Jerry bragged of his enterprise and talked about the palette of the golf course as if describing a Monet.

"There's a line of trees, a buncha elms and oaks, on Number Four fairway," he said, painting a picture. "I hit one right down the middle," he said, impressing Dad.

"There's no place better for a kid than a golf course," Dad philosophized, helping himself to a second scoop of potato salad. "It's time consuming so it keeps ya' out of trouble," Dad said, caught up in Jerry's stories, seeing him get well, hearing him sing the praises of the game, learning the language of a seasoned player.

"It's a challenge. But if you work hard at it, you'll get good," Dad said.

"Number Nine's the best," Jerry went on, chewing and talking with his mouth full. "The tee's real high. Like a mountain. You can see all the way down to the green."

He talked—Dad joined in—as if nothing bad had ever happened and never would again.

"There are a lot of things I'd rather talk about than

golf," I interrupted, bored by the conversation, impatient with Dad's sanctification of the game.

"Then maybe you should just listen," Mom suggested.

Mute, I speared my string beans, a forkful at a time, nibbling them one by one, sucking the salt and vinegar from their tips, disappearing behind the shades of my own eyes. I accepted the family's emphasis on circumstances of the moment and allowed an image to take shape in a blank space of my mind. There the past mingled with the present as in a double exposure, one focus obscuring another.

Without knowing why, my mind's eye settled on a single instance, remembering a time when I stood on the shore one late afternoon, believing that my mother would always be beside me as she was that day, her hand holding mine. I studied the water life: cattails in slow motion, lulled by the breeze. Bloated frogs formed lumps on floating lily pads; they burped when they talked. The ritual of the water bugs fascinated and perplexed; I watched them spin, one bug frantically speeding after another in a surface-only circle, stranded in a pattern, resisting the deep. The ripples radiated, then disappeared without evidence,

leaving no record that they had been there at all. I imagined the tiny creatures were without eyes, blindly obedient. What would happen if a bug defied the norm and
broke away from the immediate circle? I wondered, would
it drown?

"Why do they do that?" I asked.

"I don't know, honey," Mom answered. "Maybe they
believe that's all they can do."

Wars Laid Away

Dad had built a handsome new house on Harrison Street with a bank loan and a set of blueprints. He carted us away from 1107 Des Moines Street, a bungalow small as a depot where Mom had once tucked her kids into bunk beds at night and prayed for Dad to come home from the War, alive and in one piece. The new house with huge rooms, a fireplace and plenty of nooks and crannies felt like a castle in comparison to the cottage we had left behind. Oak floors were slicker than water slides. Steps off the kitchen wrapped around a corner and led to upstairs bedrooms, a bath, an attic, and a windowed-dormer, my dreamed-of niche with a school desk and a lake view. On stormy nights, the lake stirred outside screened windows of the bedroom Barb and I shared. On dark, still nights, I heard the water shift with the wind.

Life had begun anew on Harrison, a street with a park at the end. It seemed we had skipped a beat midsong, like a Ricky Nelson record, then started again perfectly. In reality, the past caught up with the moving van and followed the family to the next address where, undetected and insidious as smoke, history would live. In the cupboards, in the closets, in the weave of Irish linens, in the clink of silver against china dishes. In habits and rituals. Everywhere, except in the open.

Soon after we had settled in, Dad resurrected his childhood tradition, scheduling dinner in the dining room on holidays and twice during the week. Clean clothes and good manners were mandatory. Grace, recited in unison, preceded conversation that was to be civilized (Dad's word, not mine), mainly news about Dwight and Mamie and a pipe-smoking General who made headlines in the *Des Moines Register*.

"You fold the napkins," Mom said one Wednesday, the requisite weeknight. "Barb can set the table."

I shaped napkins into Lily-white tents, a prelude to dinner taught by Grandma McCarty. Before folding, I laid the cloth flat and stroked it with my fingertips, loving the feel of a damask rose embedded in fibers, sensing the subtlety of embossed threads pressed against crisp, shiny against dull. It reminded me of skating on the lake, my fingers the runners that glided over patches of choppy ice frozen into the smooth.

"Hurry up!" Barb said, appointing herself as the leader.

I folded fast, centering the silken peaks on plates, using the tail of my blouse to wipe finger prints from the china's gold rims, imagining myself to be rich as Mrs. Aster, a name I had eavesdropped when Mom hosted bridge club. I raised a dinner plate in the air, held it against the light and passed my hand behind china that was so pure it was transparent, ghostly in its beauty. Besides the silhouette of five fingers, I admired the glimpse of my face reflected in the glaze.

"You girls did a good job with the table. It's a sight for sore eyes," Mom said when she called us to dinner. "Okay, everybody. Dinner's ready."

Dad asked Dickie to lead prayers before he scooped mashed potatoes from a gold-leafed bowl that resembled a glass basket and dated back to Grandma's wedding day in another century. My favorite china piece was the gravy boat that passed around the table, clockwise—just before toilet water gushed from the chandelier and flooded the table, surprising the diners who jumped up and grabbed food from a ruined dinner.

"That damn Uncle Bill!" Dad said, backing away.

The flood had happened before. Water cascaded from the chandelier that formed a triple-tiered fountain, initiating the house many times when the toilet in the bathroom above the dining room malfunctioned. Often in front of company, bad plumbing caused an overflow, flash flooding the upstairs floor and gushing down through the chandelier, dousing the dinner table like a misguided prank.

"Uncle Bill musta' been on the sauce when he plumbed this place," Dad said. "See what you get when you give work to a drunken uncle."

Fixtures in the house tilted like Uncle Bill when he had a few under his belt, Dad said. Cold water flowed from faucets that read "hot." Faucets marked "cold" delivered scalding temperatures. Kitchen spigots sputtered and burped with water that refused to flow through clogs in the pipes. Pitying a jobless uncle, Dad had given Bill the painting and plumbing contracts on the house, though Dad had predicted Bill would drink up all his money.

Still, the rush of water through the chandelier made a glorious sight and the dining room tradition with its dangling waterfall was, to me, a time to be savored. To Dad, it was a remembrance of the peace he had brokered to quiet his war within. In a clash between the vanished luxury of his past and the duties of his present, he cherished what he had once known, holding on to beautiful but fragile things, seeing in them a dim reflection of himself, just as I had seen my face in the plate. The filligreed china, the Queen Anne table, the tinkling chandelier fed a taste for richness Dad had acquired in youth and craved in adulthood. He served pride on bone-thin plates, loving respectability, hating the haywire plumbing that, like his fate, was less than he had expected. Dad's disdain for a drunken uncle (and anyone who drank), I would one day realize, flourished in the shadow of his fear, a haunting worry that he could be counted among the shanty Irish, the less than respectable. His privileges had run out once the family's money was gone. The roadster was sold, the properties were owned by others, and Dad exchanged suits of silk for the coarse, serviceable pants of a day-laborer. Still, he worked his past into the pattern of my childhood, the ornate interwoven with the plain, like a design in Grandma's silk napkins.

The Sisters at St. Ellen's revisited our family's bygone heritage each year, threading true stories into lessons on County History Day. Sister Rega force-fed passages from George B. McCarty's handwritten journals published by the historical society. George B., Dad's grandfather, had amassed a fortune in law and land management but first, he recorded events of the town's founding. Sister said it was fitting that I read George B.'s journal entries to the class because of my connection. The story, as George B. told it, marked the end of his travel westward by team after he had crossed to America.

I struck out on my own, inching along the trail behind an Irish enclave that had claimed land along the Des Moines River in Upper Iowa, two days ride below Minnesota by wagon, I read George B.'s words to classmates who wiggled in their seats.

"Go on," Sister prodded. "I'll tell you when to stop."

The settlers had found a rich supply of timber, water, and tall grass as evidence of fertility. They settled there to tame the prairie, naming the site in honor of Irish patriot, Robert Emmet, I said. George B.'s thoughts, my voice.

After months navigating treacherous terrain, I spotted a sign of civilization, a cluster of children who spilled out of a shanty and stood in a row as if in a schoolhouse spelling bee. A herd of cows pastured near the shoreline of Battle Lake, so named by warring Indians, later called Five Island Lake by the homesteaders.

Where is Emmetsburg? I asked the children.

You are there now, sir, a small girl replied.

Yes, but where is the town?

See that stake in the grass and that one there? That is Emmetsburg.

But where is the hotel?

Oh! It's Coonan's Inn you want. It's over there, beyond the hill.

I stopped reading to clear a tickle in my throat. Then, like George B., pressed on.

On that October day in 1856, he wrote, *I made*

Emmetsburg my home and increased the town's popula-
tion to seven men, three women, and nine offspring. For
shelter, settlers have built crude cabins of logs, the bark
still on, the cracks chinked with mud, the roofs thatched
with hay and covered with sod in Irish tradition. By
Spring, nature blessed us with fish in the lake and river;
in the woods, wild duck, geese, sandhill cranes, pheas-
ant, prairie chickens, muskrats, beaver, and mink.

"Write that down," Sister interrupted. "You'll be asked
how the early settlers survived," she said to the class. To
me, "Go on. And be sure to ar-*tick*-u-late."

Crops were planted and when trappers came down
river and offered seven-thousand dollars for a winter's
catch, we praised God for the abundance of our land.
Nature's gifts compensate for extreme hardships, illnesses,
severe winters, deep snows, blistering summers, and the
fear of being slaughtered by vengeful Indians.

That was the good part of the story, vengeful Indians.
The boys stopped squirming in the seats of stone-hard
desks and started to pay attention, as if hoping see an
Indian from the real Wild West standing at the front of
the room in place of me. I read on, admiring the way

George B. told a story; his words were kind, but true, and he confessed to feeling afraid. His honesty made it seem that George B. had breathed a secret through my ear and into my brain, though I knew he was dead, buried under a tombstone in the cemetery south of town.

By the time the last of Indian land had been ceded by treaty to the United States, tribes of angry Indians roamed the land," the story said. *"A band of Sioux, the most fierce, set camp on Five Island Lake. They are so close, we can see the squaws chopping wood. Though the tribe seems peaceful and they've never tried to molest us, I am afraid.*

Again, afraid. I knew how the story ended, but the fright of my Irish-born great grandfather, a transplant on the prairie, tightened a knot of worry in my throat.

One brave rides into camp with a big club. It has a spear and a skunk tail hangs from its end, I read.

"P.U.!" the boys said. Sister, St. Ellen's oldest nun (and meanest), eyed her usual set of smart alecks when noise erupted. Since it was impossible to know which boy to blame, she issued an everyone-is-guilty command: "Sit still and listen!" she snapped, rapping her wooden ruler on a desk. The ruler with its sharp, tin strip implanted in the side was a tool of Sister's trade, along with a hotel bell parked on the corner of her desk and a clacker she carried around, squeezing it between her thumb and middle finger. Sounds Sister's students responded to were ding-ding, click-clack, and the most harsh, whack. To students, the kindest sound was the rattle of giant, wooden beads draped in the skirts worn by her religious order, Sisters of the Blessed Virgin Mary, the BVMs.

On rare occasions when she left the class alone in the room, the click of her beads in the corridor signaled her return and granted time for stray students to leap into their seats, fold their hands on their desks and, like innocent lambs, await Sister's reentry.

The center drawer in Sister's desk held a stopwatch for timing tests, a red pencil for grading, and an arithmetic book with a warning written in perfect cursive across the cover: DESK COPY. DO NOT REMOVE. I had dared to peek into it and discovered that back pages listed formulas and answers to puzzling equations. The section seemed a cheat to me—an imbalance between an adult who looked up answers and the kids she expected to figure things out.

The boys settled. Sister looked at me and, calmly, nodded for me to begin again.

The brave is a ferocious looking fellow, I said. *The Sioux are continually at war with other tribes and as they witness the onward march of the white settler on their beloved hunting ground, they grow more sullen and bitter.*

To our relief, the band broke camp before the spring thaw and moved down the Little Sioux River where they wrote a bloody page in history by slaughtering all who had settled on the shores of Spirit Lake.

I had seen the deadly spot near a cove on Spirit Lake, hating to think that blood had long ago colored the green grass a sickening red. Dad had stopped at the historic site on a summer road trip to Spirit Lake and her twin, Lake Okoboji. Anticipation of the trip, an adventure, had made me sleepless and awakened me early the morning of. Dressed in tan shorts ordered from Penney's catalogue, I skipped breakfast and claimed my place in the Fairlane. Centered in the back seat, I secured my view of the road and the chrome hood ornament, half goddess, half bird, that guided our car.

"Skootch over," Barb said when she pushed in beside me, poking my ribs with the needle of her elbow.

"Quit it!" I yelped. "You did that on purpose."

"No fightin' back there. Or we won't go," Dad warned before starting the engine.

I was almost eleven, Barb thirteen, going on fourteen. She painted her fingernails and wore lipstick, a shade called Poodle Pink, bought at the dime store with her babysitting money. At sixteen, Dickie dressed like James Dean, his hair molded into a duck tail, one greasy flounce flopping over his forehead. He rolled his T-shirt sleeves above his shoulders to display muscles that looked like braided rope. He tucked his shirttail into low-slung jeans and if he had propped a Lucky Strike like a pencil above his ear, just for show, I wouldn't have been surprised. He ignored us by staring out the window, as if denying that Barb and I were with him, sharing the back seat. Jerry, the littlest, reaped the benefits of sitting in the front between Mom and Dad.

In the front seat, Jerry twirled the dial on the radio, sliding past the Polka station from New Ulm, Minnesota, settling on baseball, the Minnesota Twins. He monitored the dashboard panel, announcing the time and rattling off the arithmetic of the miles: twenty-five miles were behind us; fifteen to go. Mom's habit was to keep Jerry close, holding his hand a lot since he had come home from the hospital. He was Mom's favorite after the fire, I thought. Not that it mattered because I saw myself as an almost-teenager, not a baby, and I was on my way to Okoboji. Dad drove west on Highway 71, past an intersection where four roads met and farmers wearing seed caps and patched overalls lounged in folding chairs while their wives tended roadside vegetable stands, hawking late garden harvests, tomatoes, onions, and green beans. Clouds above were cotton puffs. The highway connected one lingering ghost town to another, the sheds falling down and flimsy-looking, the houses thirsty for paint, the populations disappearing from once-bustling villages. The feeling that flowed into my mind, like air blowing into the car's open windows, was gratitude. So thankful was I that I didn't live in a ghost town or sell country vegetables, I said so out loud.

We passed the shore of Lost Island Lake. Still ahead lay a string of small waters, Buena Vista, Storm, and Loon lakes. Beyond the horizon, Spirit Lake and her pristine, spring-nourished sister, Lake Okoboji—the beautiful one! The two rested side by side, a narrow inlet connecting them.

The lakes were like us, Barb and me, I thought. One was grand, more gorgeous, more enchanting. One, Okoboji, got most the attention, like Barb, not me, the one with rash on her skin.

"You ridin' the roller coaster?" Barb asked for the hundredth time.

"If I don't, it's not 'cause I'm scared," I said. "It's because I don't *want* to."

"Chickie. Chickie. Chickie," she said, trying to start trouble.

"I mean it," Dad said over his shoulder, both hands on the wheel. "You kids get along."

I bounced in my seat, like a bobbin on the water. I stretched to peer through the windshield, to eye familiar landmarks, indicators of where we were, to monitor our arrival. Dad turned north at a bridge and slowed down through a town, the image of our Fairlane reflected in shop windows as we paraded by. A jog in the road bent around a curve and led us past St. Monica's church, minutes away from the lakes.

"In the name of the Father and the Son," I made the sign of the cross in front of the church, a habit instilled by the nuns.

"You think you're so holy," Barb said.

"I wish I lived here, this close to Okoboji," I said.

"I wish you did, too."

The entrance to Okoboji's amusement park arched like a rainbow, coloring the sky with hues of violet and blue. I leaned forward to see the enchantment as if for the first time. The grand entrance framed the roller coaster's spindly scaffolding that rose out of lake water. Neon lights circled the crown of Okoboji Drive-In like the rings around Saturn I had seen in my science book. Car hops in orange and black uniforms floated on roller skates, the jingle-jangle of tips—nickels and dimes—making pocket music as they balanced trays of coneys, fries, cherry cokes and chocolate malts as masterfully as butlers serving platters of party hors' d'oeuvres. In song, Elvis glorified blue suede shoes over the crackle of an outdoor loud speaker.

"I'm gettin' a summer job here—as soon as I'm old enough," Barb said. "I can skate. I can wait on cars."

Dad pulled into a gravel lot and eased between rows of cars stationed behind the Roof Garden Dance Pavilion where a playbill announced upcoming dates for Les Brown and his Band of Renown. Before we fanned out into the park, Mom spread a blanket on the grass and unpacked bologna sandwiches, two bags of Hiland potato chips, and a thermos of lime Kool-Aid. Chunks of walnut fudge and salt taffy from the Okoboji Candy Factory were promised for later though, for lunch, the picnic helped hold us to the day's limit. Five bucks apiece.

Twenty-five cents bought an all-day pass to the Fun House where I tagged behind Barb and both brothers through an entrance that blew air up my shorts from vents in the floor. Once in, the four of us tumbled like piles of pillows in the unrelenting roll of *The Barrel*. We swirled in the gravity-defying *Sugar Bowl* and, feeling queasy, I crawled out. As many times as I wanted, I hiked up stairs, narrow as a footpath, to the tip of the *Big Slide*. Using carpet remnants as a sled, I careened down the undulating hardwood that was snot slick, greasier than sleet on the VFW hill back home. Next—*The House of Mirrors, Tilt-a-Whirl* and *Bumper Cars* where Dickie and Jerry ganged up and crashed my car until I cried. They thought it was funny that I was stuck on the side of the track, jarred and bawling. Dad made them quit.

"You ridin' the roller coaster?" Barb asked again. "I'm goin' three times."

I didn't feel like answering. I didn't want to admit to fear. I had long ago been introduced to the tussle between the powers of sisterhood and the privilege of secrecy. Barb and I often coveted or tried to commandeer what the other owned, if only a piece of information. Besides, still fresh in my mind was the sour memory of the morning Sister Rega's face wrinkled and her eyes glared at me after I had wet my pants in St. Ellen's spelling bee. My skirt sopped with urine, my shoes squeaking with each step, Sister paraded me to the front of the auditorium and tried to coerce me into a confession. She prodded, promising to make me stand in the same spot all day unless I stated my shame. Sister saw that I was guilty. I didn't understand what would be accomplished by public exposure. Soggy clothes and waterlogged shoes

81

betrayed me; still, I held my right to silence. Shamefaced and head hanging, wet skirt heavy against my legs, I refused to give voice to humiliation. Sister couldn't force me to give myself away. I outlasted her and stayed mute, rigid in the stance that some secrets, however huge or small in significance, do not belong to others.

"You goin'?" Barb asked.

Looking skyward, I surveyed the situation. I heard gears crunch like the sound of bones in a bulldog's jaw as the coaster hauled itself up a hill. Passengers shrieked, then plunged into a valley, the rattletrap cars splashing into lake water on a low-lying dip, triggering a reflex in me. I felt on the verge of vomiting.

"What do you think?" Dad asked "Do you want to go?"

I froze.

All my life, Dad had occupied our house and dominated the household, though it seemed he ruled from a distance. Evenings after work, he hid his mood behind the *Register & Tribune*, listening while reading, peering over eyeglasses, talking from behind the rustle of open pages, if he talked at all. He was there, but not there.

Other times, he communicated in an unspoken way, rescuing the underdog with hardly a word, the protector of dignity, public confession not required.

"I'll go with you," Dad said, gathering my fingers like dandelions in his palm.

We walked up the ramp and climbed into a car, a red and yellow one. Dad tightened the strap on the seat and I wrapped my hands around his arm, my face buried in his shoulder to avoid looking at the track. My hair floated in the wind like weeds in water when we hit the downhill. I latched on tighter to Dad, sucked in my breath and flew, unafraid.

The last batch of tickets was saved for the day's finale, a sunset cruise on The Okoboji Queen. We glided over blue-white waves on the west shoreline and from the upper deck, Dad pointed out the Manhattan Beach property that had been built by George B. The forty-room bayside estate dignified the women and children who had summered there. They came alive in my imagination. I saw crowds congregating on the lawn for games of croquet and Sunday picnics of smoked ham, fried chicken, potato salad, and slices of iced watermelon. Men who motored out for the weekends wore straw boaters with striped hat bands; women wore bonnets, pink magnolias weighing down the brims. On the wrapped verandah, ladies dressed in organdy or tulle; jeweled combs held their hair. A breeze waltzed across the lake and came to visit through the screen on an ornamental door, welcome as an invited guest. I had heard of these people in family folklore; I had seen them in vintage photos, their turn-of-the-century elegance preserved in sepia, images of Dad's mother and aristocratic grandmother summering in bonnets and gowns.

"The McCarty's had piles of money," Dad reminded us, as he had many times. "And they lost it. They pissed it away during the Depression," he said, acrimoniously. "They pissed away every dime."

Dad's stories felt darker than Mom's, as if he hadn't learned to rewrite the endings. In youth, he had been narrow-faced and thin-lipped, his hair parted in the middle, slicked back on the sides, dapper. He had spent summers on Lake Okoboji and drove a Buick when he escorted Mom to Electric Park and danced to the Champagne Orchestra led by Lawrence Welk, an accordion player from South Dakota. Mom romanced us with re-membrances of whirling around a lakeside ballroom under the stars, spinning tales of her life as a country girl in love with a rich boy who lived in a big house in town. Before we were born.

After cruising on the Okoboji Queen, Dad ushered us back to the car and drove along the shoreline, then pulled into a rest area for a lesson of the past.

"Here's the spot," Dad said, opening car doors and rousting us out. We formed a semicircle around an historic marker, the toes of Barb's wedgies and my sandals pointing like arrows toward a boulder set on the sod where blood had been shed a century ago. In the background, gulls skimmed blue water and sailboats pocketed the wind, disguising the lake's tortuous history. Bolted to the stone, a commemorative engraving carried a cryptic message:

Spirit Lake Massacre

March 8, 1857

Here lie the forty men, women and children who were

brutally murdered on the ill-fated day when

Inkpadutah and his band of Sioux invaded the
peaceful and happy
settlement of Spirit Lake, murdering all.
After holding their war dance,
Inkpadutah and his ferocious followers painted bloody
signs of victory upon the smoothed surface of a tree
and moved on to fresh fields.

"There was only one survivor. A little girl," Dad said.
"It was Inkpadutah that George B. saw riding into camp.
It could have been your great grandfather and all of
Emmetsburg that was wiped out. We wouldn't be stand-
ing here."

Night inked the surroundings, erasing the day as Dad
drove us home. Pity the poor settlers, I thought. How
could they have sailed away from what had been familiar, from what they had loved, their home soil? And then
be killed for it. Why had they come to America, I wondered. For land and opportunity, Sister had said. For freedom, Barb had said, as if she knew everything. Your daddy
fought for your freedom, too. And don't you kids ever
forget it, Mom added. I had not traveled far: once to

Bemidji, Minnesota, to stare at the statue of Paul Bunyan and Babe, the Blue Ox. Twice to Ontario on Dad's fishing expeditions. Each summer to Okoboji. Far enough to know I would never leave home, never have war, never leave the lake, never leave family. And never would I want them to leave me.

The rhythm of tires on the road hummed me into a state of sleepiness. I slumped, my head flopped like Raggedy Ann on Barb's shoulder until we were aroused by the smell of a skunk someone had run over in the dark. We rolled up car windows for protection, but the musk seeped in, saturated the air, stung tired eyes, and trailed us for miles. The memory of it made the sheets smell extra sweet when, once home, I skipped prayers and crawled into bed, still wearing shorts and sandals.

I asked Mom if I could leave the hall light burning to keep the dark from creeping over me.

"Why do you hafta have the light on?" Barb asked. She always asked, but I never told.

Deep inside, I had buried the cause, one too horrible to tell. It wasn't fear of the unknown; it was the sweeping terror of a certainty, an unthinkable dread planted by the melancholy of an old Celtic song I had heard Grandma sing from her rocking chair while she darned socks one afternoon:

Angels came in the night as I lay sleeping, the song said.

And they took my mother away.

If darkness never came, I reasoned, neither would the angels. I thought I heard the thrum of their wings outside the bedroom window, but it was an owl flying in the pitch of midnight. I tangled in sheets, suspended in sensations; the day's images tumbled, one over another like bodies tossing in the Fun House barrel. Cookie trotted into the room, looking for a sleep mate. She positioned her paws on the edge of the bed and with a hop, hauled her hindquarters up, snuggling in, her tummy whirring against my ribs. She whimpered out of neediness, out of having been abandoned earlier in the day.

"Don't worry, Cookie. Everybody's home. Safe and sound," I said. Her coat glistened in the glow of a light in the hall. Half adrift, my head heavy on the pillow, a jumble of fears, worries, hopes, and memories streamed into dreams yet to be. Once more, I trailed my hand through the scruff of Cookie's neck and beneath my fingertips, I detected a tiny bump on her hide buried in the fur. I believed it to be a flea.

The Last Mansion

Plans stretched out over time, like a jail break. Kids congregated under the lamplight and swapped whispered strategies on the street corner. There was a ringleader, Dickie. The scheme was to round up a small band of renegades, mostly boys, and on the last Saturday before school, mobilize.

Besides swimming, the Fourth of July, and a trip to Okoboji, summertime offered one other plum event: breaking into the Van Gordon mansion.

The gang met that day down by the swimming dock and headed to Van Gordon's, an adventure granted to chosen ones who swore to keep a secret for the rest of their lives, the few who were brave enough to sneak in, inching through overgrown weeds. We parked our bikes at the bathhouse as decoys and, from there, traveled on foot. Covert, we snaked along little-traveled paths and parted head-high reeds along the east lake shore as we passed. We hit the dirt and crawled on our stomachs, undetectable as worms, bodies gliding through uncut grass once we reached the Van Gordon property line. Dickie popped his head up periodically, checking to see if Sheriff Miller's patrol car was circling the block.

In a decayed backyard garden, a statue of St. Francis of Assisi posed, his crumbling hands clasped in prayer. A ring of hair rimmed his stone head as if it were a halo and a bluebird, stone-silent, perched on his shoulder. At St. Francis' feet, shattered tiles from a fish pond hinted of former luxury. Dickie removed a cardboard covering from a window that had been smashed by a rock and, feet first, we took turns shimmying through. A jagged edge on the glass sliced Jimmy Fitzpatrick's T-shirt and drew a bloody line, a badge of courage, across his collar bone. He winced, but he didn't whine. Inside, dollops of dust poufed like smoke in a sorcerer's spell as everyone tumbled, one by one, onto the basement's dirt floor.

We were in!

"Take a count!" Dickie said. "Be sure everyone made

it."

The basement, hot and airless, smelled putrid as great-grandma Gallagher's fish stew and buckwheat gravy. For all I knew, it was the stench of dead bodies buried there. The odor hit me, and I felt it was a mistake for me to be in on the action. I fumbled to find Barb's hand in the dark and I held on hard. Automatically, the string of raggedy neighborhood kids connected like convicts in a chain gang, the biggest and boldest first: Dickie, followed by Fitzpatrick, Sack Norvell, Spider Spies, Wimp Rutledge, Barb, and the littlest, me. We felt our way along the rough stones and crumbled mortar of the basement wall, slinking forward. A veil of cobwebs fingered my face in a conspiracy with fear and darkness that made me numb and struck me speechless. My eyes darted around, cobwebs everywhere.

"I'm scared," I whispered, my voice rediscovered.

"*Shut Up!* Everybody be quiet!" Dickie said.

Breathing stopped. The air didn't move, but it stunk. Everyone crouched, listening. For cops. For ghosts. For rats scratching. For anything, dead or alive.

"Okay." Dickie issued the all-clear. We breathed free

again.

"I want to go *home*," I begged.

"You wanted to come. And you're stayin'," Dickie said.

The miracle was that I had been included in the first place. My reputation as a tattletale had tagged me beyond the halls of St. Ellen's, so I bargained, buying my way into the circle with packs of candy cigarettes and a vow of eternal secrecy.

"Don't be scared," Barb said. "Stay together."

Her hand looped mine. She squeezed my fingers until they hurt. I couldn't blame her if she was scared, too. The nuns at St. Ellen's classified sins as venial or mortal; crime and misdemeanors were other matters. We knew without saying it that breaking and entering meant violating the law. In secret, I liked that Barb took chances along with the boys, making tough decisions while I eased into the comfort of not needing to be strong. At times, our extremes were complimentary like when at Christmas, red goes with green.

"Look it," Barb said. "See! There's light comin' from under the door," she said, excited as if she had found gold.

Daylight poured pure as spring water under a crack at the top of the stairs. Dust particles drifted in the stream.

"We only have a coupla' steps to go." She portioned out assurance, though I wondered whether she had led me toward something wonderful or drawn me deep into trouble.

"Stay beside me. We're almost there."

The steps bowed under our weight, their creak the only sound as Barb and I scaled the stairs on hands and knees, following the boys. Dickie, first to finish the climb to the top, thrust the door open with his shoulder and let warm, welcome light wash into the basement. We peered into the kitchen, a room as vast as a pond, but otherwise not extraordinary. Only odd. A brass tea pot on the grate of a gas-burning stove sat cold and forgotten beside a Kelvinator that had stopped humming. Dishes were stacked like cake layers in the sink. Tea had evaporated and left its stain in a cup. Chairs were strewn. Open-winged pages of *The Wall Street Journal* spread over the table with news that had grown stale. *Cream of Wheat*, withered and browned, looked like sand in the bottom of breakfast bowls.

"Taste it," Fitzpatrick said.

"I'm not tastin' it," Dickie said.

For years, the place had sat abandoned, its contents left behind, its owners missing. The reason was unknowable; the mystery, a charm. For once, I had been granted secret passage to see the incomprehensible with my own eyes. There was no turning back.

"Come on. I'll show you somethin'," Dickie said.

Again, he led. We followed him up three steps, across a portal-landing, into a formal parlor, a dust-covered shrine to wealth and industry lit by sunlight that filtered through window grime. A grand piano posed on fluted, feminine legs, its teeth once gleaming in ebony and white, representing the Rockefeller-style lives that had been led in that house, in that room.

I was an instant impresario. I rushed to the piano and pounced on the keys, pounding out a concert of powerful non-chords which were to me a rhapsody, an interlude inserted in an afternoon. Despite inexperience, I recognized a sign of respectability in a single word etched in gold above the keys: Steinway.

The boys sprang to action all around. Dickie, the tallest, stood on a chair to reach a rack of sabers mounted on an oak-paneled wall. He entrusted two blades to his companions, noblemen then, reserving the most beautiful sword for himself, wiping dust from the sheath on his pant leg. The boys gripped the handles above golden cross guards, like D'Artagnan might have done, and with their left hands, slid the sharp, steely tongues from jeweled sheaths—princely, kingly things. They clashed impetuously, challenging one another to duels, creating high adventure with the flashing souvenirs of some ancient society. *Swisssh! Whoooosh!* They sliced the air. They jumped, lunged, deflected death and, hands held over hearts, fell on Van Gordon's parlor floor.

Being there was better than being in a movie.

Concerns then seemed immaterial. Adventure trumped the law; the thrill of risk absorbed a sense of apprehensive guilt. Fun out-balanced fear. Still, I glanced up from my fantasy to study a portrait of old P.F. Van Gordon boxed in a gilded frame and mounted above the mantel. He was tuxedoed and wax-mustached in oil paint, his hand inserted into a buttoned vest as if he were Napoleon. I needed to see if his eyes had moved since the last time I looked.

By then, Barb had bee-lined to a second-floor bed-room, rich with belongings of the blue-blooded Van Gordon girl.

"Come upstairs!" Barb called to me, yelling down the stairs. "Get up here and see what I found!"

She had surrounded herself with furs snatched from the closets: a sable coat, a mink wrap, a full-length fox, a muskrat jacket and a curly Persian lamb with raglan sleeves and shoulder pads. The room had cast its spell over her: she tried to wear all the furs at once, piling the full-lengths over the cape. I rummaged through trunks splashed with stickers from steamship lines that had once docked in exotic ports and found my style in a diamond tiara, a peach-colored ball gown, and layers of lace hidden within. Imagining myself Cinderella, I dressed in a strapless gown that poured into a soft puddle of silk on the floor. On me, everything liquified. Wobbling on three-inch heels strapped to my ankles like stilts, tiara teetering, I waded through the silken pool at my feet. A crocheted shawl washed over chicken-bone shoulders and a string of pearls cascaded from a scrawny neck. Jewels dripped from my ears. Lipstick, the color of cranberries at Thanksgiving, slid off the corners of my mouth and dribbled onto my chin. A cheval mirror standing next to an armoire captured my image. I was a vision.

Dolls with rosy cheeks and cherub faces were tossed among mounds of lace pillows, like flower petals scattered by rain. I bounced on the canopy bed, then lifted the lid on a silver music box that had been left under the shade of a stained-glass lamp on a doilied night stand. I poked my nose into its innards as if expecting the tune to be wearing perfume. I imagined what it might be like to own a prized possession like a music box, to steal it, to wind it up and hide it under my pillow, its tinkling music lingering in the night. A collection of hand-painted figurines and bells of glistening porcelain sat in a straight row on a shelf across the room, needing to be touched. A filigreed jewelry case hid a studded cross on a tarnished chain, buried among pearl beads and piles of earrings, rings and rubies, brooches, cameo pins, and jeweled clusters.

"Don't break anything," Barb said, snuffing my temptations. "This isn't ours, you know."

Once costumed—I in bias-cut silk and my sister in animal skins—we ventured downstairs to find an audience. Two princesses descended, pausing midway on the curved staircase to strike a pose, to reign over the parlor with arched doorways that were dressed, fancy as we, in stained glass and wooden frets that looked like spider webs spun into corners. There beneath ceiling murals, the boys swashbuckled among imported vases on carved pedestals.

There had been occasional Van Gordon sightings, none verified. A local businessman claimed he had spotted Van Gordon living in comfort under an assumed name in Chicago's Conrad Hilton Hotel without his wife and children (which prompted a search for bodies in the mansion's backyard). Dad and other avowed Republicans cast Van Gordon, a staunch Democrat, as a man who had developed a habit of borrowing money without paying it back. The old mogul fell into financial trouble with the IRS, they reasoned. Others imagined the family had booked a cruise and were swept away at sea. Or they all went crazy and were sent to the insane asylum.

One theory involved aliens. To hear Grandma tell it,

she saw the whole startling incident with her own eyes: Mr. and Mrs. Van Gordon and their twin children, Clara and Cole, out on a Sunday drive, paused at the railroad tracks near the cemetery to wait for a passing train. Without warning, a whirling, saucer-shaped object sliced through the sky and hovered like a bird over water. As suddenly as it appeared, the silver thing swooped and sucked up Van Gordon's 1948, two-toned blue Packard with the family still in it. All that was left was a moonfaced crater in the road and a blinding beam of light.

Had the Van Gordons left clues to the truth of their disappearance, we didn't unearth them while sifting through the treasures of their rooms. Near night, Dickie jolted us with a sudden command:

"We gotta get outa here, you guys. Mom and Dad will be lookin' for us," he said.

I dashed to the piano for an encore to a swell of imagined applause. The boys repositioned sabers on wall racks and Barb folded dresses, packed them in trunks on layers of lace, bedded the jewels on velvet trays, and returned furs to hangers in the closet. Like the Van Gordons, we abandoned the house and its contents, fleeing, taking nothng along. We left the way we had come, in the musk of the basement, out through a broken window.

The summer after, a court declared the Van Gordon family legally dead. Dick Martin, town mortician, paid three-thousand dollars in back taxes at a sheriff's auction on the steps of the courthouse square and bought the mansion he could barely see under its shroud of seventeen Elm trees. Martin's picture ran on the front page of the *Reporter* when he bought the property. He beamed from the prim Victorian verandah before he ordered the mansion torn down to make way for the Martin Funeral Home, turning the house to a pile of broken bones. I took comfort in her passing, having known the place in my own way—privately, since I had sworn never to reveal her secrets. The mansion, to me, was a gracious town dowager, once stunning and rich. Finding neighborhood kids in the house, she entertained in the parlor and, though they were uninvited, she made her guests feel grand, telling her tale without a word spoken, stringing the beads of her story in colors and smells, textures and sounds, leaving the whole of truth to imagination. Others of her station had passed. Of the old mansions pointed out to me in childhood, only two still lingered in their dotage, decrepit and difficult to maintain, their porches hacked, their rooms cut into kitchenettes.

"I got the old girl for a heckuva price," Martin told the newspaper with a hint of pride, not sorrow. "The amazing thing is, there in the parlor was the grand piano with not a scratch on it. I sat down and played it. All it needed was a tuning."

League of Women

Mom went to work at the bowling alley. She earned thirty-five dollars a week, less than thirty after deductions. Other mothers, non-working mothers—namely, Harriet O'Connell—considered Mom's behavior to be disgraceful. Harriet told me so.

Mary Kate O'Connell and I, chums from St. Ellen's, had busied an August afternoon by squeezing pieces into a picture puzzle, three boats tossing on a white-capped sea. We were sprawled on Mary Kate's bedroom floor, snacking on saltines and mayonnaise, when Harriet nabbed me. She ushered me into her living room, settled me in the middle of a Queen Anne love seat (purple velvet) and wiggled in beside me, a cigarette in one hand and a cocktail in the other.

"You would be so much better off if your mother

would stay home and take care of you," she said. She swirled the ice cubes in her glass, the crystals clinking in an afternoon cocktail, one of many Harriet downed before dinner. At our house, the evening meal was called supper; it was dinner at theirs.

"It's an awful shame," she said. "You kids home alone."

I felt a rush like a hot blast scorching my face and ears—humiliation, it must have been. Out of the corner of one eye, I noticed O'Connell's housekeeper puttering in the music room across the hall, dusting baubles, picking them up and putting them down in the same place, swishing piano keys with a cotton cloth. And I caught Mary Kate peeking around the door jam, trying to listen. Harriet, her legs tan and narrow, her hair twisted into a knot at the top of her head, examined me with the dark coals of her eyes. Not knowing what to say, I stared back, dumbstruck, studying her face as if it were a rouge-blotched painting, the canvas of her skin cracked from sunny days on the golf course. I disliked Harriet a lot for saying something mean about my mother. But I was glad of one thing.

The big relief was that Harriet had her clothes on. It was normal for her to parade around the house bare naked after sunning herself like a lizard out on the lawn. My brother Jerry pretended to be Patrick O'Connell's buddy, conning Patrick, begging for a drink of Kool Aid on hot days, finagling an invitation into O'Connell's kitchen to peer into the light of an open refrigerator, his eyes darting, hoping to catch sight of a nude Harriet trotting through the rooms. I had witnessed her nakedness many times, her body as spindly as a sapling that had its leaves whipped off by a hard wind. I had pretended not to notice, diverting my eyes after one good look, behaving as if everyone's Mom disrobed and roamed the house, a snifter of whiskey in their hand.

"I better go now," I said. "Thank you for inviting me," I added, out of habit.

I pointed my feet toward home, purposeful in my stride, careful to avoid the sidewalk's dividing lines—*step on a crack, you'll break your mother's back.* I marched along the pathway beneath a church-like ceiling of elms on Harrison Street, beyond O'Connell's house, past neighboring yards and rows of red maples, walnut and apple trees. Normally, I liked the comfort of relying on others to make my decisions, letting someone else be strong. But that afternoon, it was as if an inner muscle had strengthened. I honored my thoughts, not Harriet's. I resolved to protect my mom from Harriet's zing and arrow. I would pocket Mrs. O'Connell's comment and I would wipe Mary Kate off my slate of friends with her mother's spiteful smear. Our schoolgirl friendship, Mary Kate's and mine, would be sacrificed, I decided, not in a spirit of anger, but in fake indifference, a kind of sixth-sense defense that came naturally to a sixth-grade girl. When school started, I would ask Sister to move me away from Mary Kate even if it meant sitting in the front row next to Ronald Gruber whose pants smelled like manure from farm chores. What I didn't expect was that Ginger would side with Mary Kate, doubling my loss, my best friend remaking herself as my enemy. I would be friendless as usual through most of the year, wobbling on the shaky leg of principle. Mrs. O'Connell disapproved of my mom; in turn, I disapproved of her. Mary Kate and Ginger disapproved of me. Disapproval all around. It was complicated.

The year was 1955. A complicated time.

Unpaid bills had piled up at our house in the stretch of time since Jerry had come home from the hospital. Dad took to playing poker at Hamilton's Tap until long after midnight, not phoning home, trying to earn a pot of money, losing money instead. Humiliation had driven him to the game table in the pool hall after an unknown man, imposing in a brown tweed overcoat, rang the front doorbell and stepped into our living room. How did Dad plan to pay past-due medical bills, the man demanded to know.

Mom shuttled the kids into the kitchen, out of earshot. I overheard few details of the confrontation in the living room, but in a figment of my imagination, worry hovered. What if the Cagney-type stranger in a Fedora pulled a gun out of his vest and shot my Dad because of money, like in the movies. I felt an uneasiness, a sense that something was really, really wrong.

It was deep winter, January. Night fell before five o'clock in the afternoons; temperatures fell, too, and Dad receded into a silent state, a "stew," Mom called it. He had fought a war and never spoke of it. He had quit smoking cigarettes and never spoke of it. He did not drink alcohol, not a drop, and never spoke of it. But the press of debt buried him in a troublesome silence, pride and tattered pedigree no match for the night the doorbell chimed and The Collector stepped through the door to ask an unanswerable question.

Mom cried that night and cried again in a string of evenings when dad stayed late at the tavern, his chair empty at the supper table, his side of the bed unmussed, silence his chosen ally. It seemed that once Mom started to cry, she might never stop until, finally dry-eyed, she gathered us, Dad too, around the kitchen table to make an announcement.

"I got a job! I'm going to run the bowling alley," she said, not asking, but telling. "I'm the new manager."

Everyone stopped eating. Eyes widened.

"Nobody's mom works," Barb said, her voice the same as a heckle, Mom in the glare of center stage.

My mind flipped into an automatic inventory: Ginger's mom stretched on her sofa, perpetually horizontal, her hair, red-mixed-with-gray, matted on a pillow, an open book propped in her hands. She ran their household from a reclining position, directing the housekeeper, sending Ginger to Carney's Corner Grocery to buy steamed Halibut and broccoli for their supper. I had hardly ever seen Ginger's mother upright, unless she was going golfing. Mary Kate O'Connell's mom didn't work. Mary Jo Ryan's mother didn't work, though she took in ironing and laundry and starched the ruffles on Mary Jo's pinafores until they stood on her shoulders, jaunty as plumes on an old-fashioned pen, drawing admiration from the nuns. Beaver Cleaver's mother, a model housewife hovering in a pinched-waist frock and dress shoes, tended to duties—cookies that needed to be baked (I could smell chocolate chips through the TV), pillows that needed to be fluffed, homework The Beave needed to do when he came home from school, a dinner table that needed to be properly set. I imagined the appliances in Mrs. Cleaver's spotless kitchen in the color of avocado green, like in *Good Housekeeping* magazine.

The only mother I knew who worked outside the home was Mrs. Pierrat. A war widow, mother of Roger Pea Rat, she waited on customers at Hughes Drugstore to buy food and pay rent in one of the old McCarty mansions that had been sectioned off and made into apartments. She had no husband, Roger had no father, and they had no real house to live in. I knew they were poor; a cinder drive ran past their apartment, but there was no car to park. It felt strange, thinking my mom would go to work like Roger Pea Rat's mom.

"It looks like a man can't take care of his family," Dad said, his lips tightening over his teeth until his mouth turned white like it had frost around it. I could see that, to Dad, what mattered was not what people said, but what he feared they might say. He nudged his food with a fork and examined his plate. I wondered what fish sticks and green peas looked like through Dad's eyes. I had often felt thankful that I had not been born color blind like he was, grateful that I had not missed seeing a plum's purple skin or the glow of a peach, its scarlet heart revealed beneath tooth marks in the pulp. I felt sorry that Dad could distinguish only shades of gray in his unwonderful world without color, as if doomed to always see shadows.

"I can't just sit around and cry any more," Mom said. When I looked again at her, it seemed like a spark had been set off, tears had dried, hope and anticipation lit her face, her glow so different from Dad's, her spunk having sprung from hard, fertile soil. As the oldest in her family—five girls; the sixth, a boy—gritty farm chores, far more indelicate than gathering eggs the hens laid in the chicken coop, had landed squarely on the shoulders of Mom's childhood. One challenge renewed itself each spring when the run off from winter snows caused the creek to rise. It was Mom, the oldest, who led a rescue crew, recruiting two sisters to help row a boat through fields swollen with floodwaters and save the stranded animals from near-drowning and hunger. The three girls would wrestle baby pigs into the boat, bind them with a rope to keep them aboard, and row them, squealing, back to dry land and safety. Mom also took charge of the old grandfather who, by the time he died at the age of ninety-six, had lived with the family ten years, his bed, a cot set in a corner of an upstairs bedroom, icy cold in winter, hellish in summer. He had crossed to America as a boy, a sickly child, who would have been thrown overboard had he died, Mom said. She told (and retold) tales of a grandfather who disguised himself with a long, gray beard and a scowl and spoke not a word of English. His nose had grown bulbous and purple, she said, like a small water balloon aquiver on his face.

"He was in his Second Childhood," she explained. "And he scared me half to death."

The grandfather, Mom remembered, laid sleepless through deep nights, chanting the Catholic Mass in Latin, over and over, filling the house with a mournful sound of psalms after sundown. When he wandered away in a blizzard, the family feared frostbitten limbs and lungs locked in pneumonia. A search party branched out across a frozen acreage, trudging through snow drifts, knee-deep, until Mom heard the Kyrie Eleison pouring out of a haystack, in Latin. Pulled from the hay pile, the old man was led into the house and warmed near the belly of a wood-burning stove, his feet planted in a tub of scalding water, a shot of Southern Comfort as tonic. Mom rubbing his bones riled him and he bolted up, threw off the blankets, and chased her through the kitchen with the butcher knife Grandma used to whack off the butt end of a ham—the first, though not the last, time he terrorized her with a blade, sending her scurrying and quaking beneath the kitchen table. The scene, as Mom told it, set a stage in my mind for an old-time adventure packed with excitement and suspense—a grandpa gone wild, armed and perilous, blithering in native tongue, Mom cast as the damsel who saved herself, outwitting danger.

"That's just the way it was," she said, wrapping up her stories. "Back then, everyone took care of their own. You do what you have to do in life," she said. "Simple as that."

No discussion followed Mom's decision to take a job, though anyone looking to Dad for a sign of approval needed to search elsewhere. He wasn't alone in adjusting; I, too, had loved having Mom home in the pre-bowling alley days. Especially missed were sewing experiments that manufactured my clothes. I had apprenticed when Mom outfitted me in a princess-style coat fashioned from pink boucle' and a Butterick pattern. As usual, the pin cushion was missing and Mom, the improviser, laid the pattern on the dining room floor and held pieces in place with—anything.

"Bring a couple more coffee cups," she said, directing me from a position on the floor.

She crawled over the fabric on hands and knees and smoothed out pattern pieces that were meant to be sleeves, bodices, and panels for a bias-cut skirt; I delivered objects collected from around the house, kitchen cupboards mainly. By the time she finished—the pattern anchored by cups, saucers, soup bowls, and a dinner plate—it looked like she had spread a picnic on the hardwood floor.

"See!," she said. "Who needs pins?"

She matched seams and pressed them with her fingertips, stitched the parts together on a Singer, then sent me to parade down the center aisle before an Easter Sunday audience, the faithful at St. Thomas. I listened to wrens twittering in the trees, renewing their tribute to the glory of morning, as I walked to church by myself in a prima-donna moment, imagining that the birds' trill was for me. I met Ginger on the corner by the church, the Peter Pan collar on my new coat laying off-kilter, the buttons missing because Mom didn't get around to tacking them on. Still, Mom's craftsmanship had set me apart from those who, like Ginger, wore store-bought clothes and Mom's fashion sense was equal to a prophecy: "You'll be the envy of all the girls, including the nuns," she had predicted.

True, Sister Rega remarked on the special quality of my coat—*thank you, Sister, my mom made it*—when I dipped my finger in the bowl of holy water in the church vestibule, my hand gliding through the sign of the cross, the hem of the boucle' brushing the kneeler when I genuflected, the Easter miracle being that Sister signaled a secret jealousy since she, the chaste, was not allowed the worldliness of wearing pink, like me.

Home sewing was, sadly, among the projects abandoned in the empty, hollowed-out atmosphere that enveloped the house when Mom went to work. Especially in the beginning, I felt the unease of a divided politic in a household gripped by opposing philosophies—Dad uncooperative, Mom undeterred and I, unable to judge what was right and who was wrong. Sorting through my feelings reminded me of sifting through a treasury of old photographs—who were these people? Scenes and faces came into focus from before—when they were young, when they were smiling, when we settled on Five Island's sandy shore, the Fourth of July fireworks flashing like cancans in the ballroom of the sky, sparks whirling down to the lake's mirrored surface, sizzling before dissolving in the water's darkness, their glory gone. Memories registered clearly, though a vision of tomorrow was cloudy in my mind. I could not picture the future with an absent Mom and a sulking Dad, nor could I imagine how or when, if ever, the family's next photographic moments would appear.

Then the newspaper announced the date that six lanes would be readied for bowling: three nights and one day a week. Wednesdays were reserved for league play with open bowling on Friday nights and Saturdays. Family rates made Sunday afternoons a draw—all bowling over in time for six o'clock supper and the Ed Sullivan Show. Non-school nights, Jerry and I were enlisted to keep score for bowlers who suffered from bad eyesight or were troubled by arithmetic. Practicing math, we penciled pin counts into squares on the score sheet, tallying strikes and spares, carrying the numbers over for a grand total, counting on our fingers, feeling good to be in on the game. The balls were too heavy to lift, but I liked to dust my fingers with chalk and run my palms over the baldness of a twelve-pound ladies' Brunswick, my favorite a magenta flecked with gold, a magnificent bead in a string of plain colored balls of black and forest green.

Dickie—nicknamed Mac by then—quickly earned a paycheck and a title: assistant manager in charge of mopping the lanes, selling fountain drinks, malts and cherry cokes, closing the night register, and taking deposits to the bank. Without a food license or kitchen facility, Mom brought ham sandwiches from home and sold them over the counter, carting bottles of ketchup and jars of mustard, mayonnaise and pickles in a purse slung over one shoulder. She laid out the food and the condiments and dumped bags of potato chips on a paper plate, free with every sandwich. Tall as the countertop, I stood by and watched Mom unpack her groceries for ravenous bowlers, intrigued by the rabbits she pulled out of the hat, though I had seen most her tricks before.

Sometimes, I was promoted to the malt-making job. The recipe, easy: globs of vanilla ice cream, chocolate syrup and powdered malt tossed into an aluminum canister and shoved under a mixer to whirrrrrrrrr into a froth, creamier than Ice-ees from the Dairy Queen, thick enough to clog a straw.

It was Barb, though, who struck economic and social gold. She pocketed ten cents a lane as the first girl to be a pin boy. Tall as a man, she measured nearly six feet before graduating St. Ellen's and her long-fingered grab raked up three pins at a time. Skinny and nimble, she jumped in and out of the pit, agile as any athlete. Her face splatted with freckles (mine patched with outbreaks of eczema), Barb yanked her hair into a pony tail and rolled up the cuffs on her Levi's to show off white socks, same as the pair she stuffed in her bra to wow the bowling-alley boys. Her circle grew as her poodle-skirted friends swarmed and swooned over top-tier celebrities, Dickie's high school buddies who enlivened the place— Shorty Lowe, Poop Prochaska, Lornie, and His Cool-ness, Babe Fisher, a borderline hoodlum who twisted his hair into a blonde spit curl that wormed its way down his forehead. Coveted in a new Ford Fairlane, the Babe drove Barb and her friends crazy, honking at them as he wheeled around town in his two-tone coupe, hot pink and white, eyeing them when he strolled through the bowling alley door like a gunslinger stepping into the saloon, hearts of the dance hall girls aflutter.

Ginger made up with me, too. She joined the hoop-di-do with her brothers, Soupie and Hootie. They played poker at a collapsible table in the front before the bowlers came in; Barb's crowd jammed the juke box, swinging their skirts to the rock-n-roll rhythm of Bill Haley and the Comets on Decca Records; Ginger and I slid down long, glassy lanes in stocking feet, Mom warning not to scratch the alleys with the rivets on our jeans. She taped a handwritten sign to the wall:

NO SHENANIGANS

The place reeked of dust, oil and sweat and yet, it somehow smelled sweet as a high school gymnasium in basketball season. The thunder of balls loping down hard-wood lanes (or gutters) underscored Chubby Checker records spinning on the juke box and pumped up the tempo of the small world I had lived in. Before, familiar planets had been three: home, school, and church; role models, women who baked and delivered cream pies to the altar society or women like Harriet who took an af-ternoon nip.

"Come on! Get your shoes on," Mom prompted, one

Saturday morning. "You can come with me, if you want."

"Where're we goin'?" I asked, abandoning my job—licking Green Stamps, the taste of glue accumulating on the buds of my tongue, the stamps stuffing the pages of premium books, my head jammed with dreams of trading the stamps for prizes, radios, watches, pots and pans. REDEEM—was the word the stamp people used.

"I'm giving some bowling lessons this morning," Mom said. "Hop in the car and let's go."

Assigned to a seat within reach of the score pad, I sat up straight to reach the tabletop. From there, I watched the action, studying the style Mom taught to a bevy of women bowlers who rented tri-patterned shoes and wore teal-colored, gabardine shirts with the name of their team—Emmetsburg Plumbing and Heating—lettered in gold across their backs. Positioned on the runway, Mom raised her right arm, supporting the ball in the palm of her hand, holding it aloft as if it were weightless as a plum pulled from a pie, her thumb stuck in it.

"Hold the ball high as your chin," she instructed, lifting the Brunswick in demonstration.

"Keep your eye on the ten pin," she said.

She turned with the precision of a dancer, facing the lane, moving forward—focused, yet graceful and strong—approaching her challenge not with a leap, but in small, measured steps, a sort of glissade. She targeted the set of pins and showed the ladies how to smooth out the back swing and thrust the ball. She released the ball to the boards, showing finesse, spiraling it perfectly down the center of the alley, hitting the king pin with a thwack!— a blow powerful enough to pit the lacquer and send all pins reeling, their hard, wooden veneer no more intimidating to Mom than old, established attitudes she had tossed to the high heavens, reeling, tumbling, landing in a heap to be picked up, reset and regrouped by someone's daughter, frame after frame, adding up to a brand new game.

"Strike!" Mom yelled when the pins went flying. I believed Mom could win money on Championship Bowling broadcast on TV, if they let women play.

"Way to go!," said the ladies, whooping and screaming.

With each consecutive strike (and spare), the women jumped up and down, bobbing and clapping like junior-high cheerleaders. I leaped out of my seat and squealed, too—a natural impulse because, for once, I felt like an important part of the team. It was not me sitting on the sidelines, as usual; it was me keeping up and keeping score for a new league of women who dressed in monogrammed shirts and rented shoes. It seemed like the most unlonely moment I had ever known; I liked the feeling. In fact, I wondered what it might be like to live at the bowling alley.

All that had happened by the time Harriet O'Connell's husband ran off, abandoning Harriet and six kids—two of his, two of hers, and two they had together. Her husband was discovered years later, living under an assumed name in Kansas City—a bigamist, some said—selling shoes at a store next to Macy's on Petticoat Lane, cattycorner from where Harry Truman's haberdashery had been. Harriett went to work, too, peddling home appliances in the store she had inherited from her dead parents. With little opportunity for golf or sunning, she joined the women's Wednesday night bowling league and kept her clothes on the whole time.

In the Kingdom of Childhood

A commotion in the street behind the house halted breakfast and the family streamed out of the kitchen, bowls of
oatmeal cooling on the table. We synchronized into a line
along bay windows in the dining room to witness what
had happened. Through sunlit glass, I saw Susie crumpled
under the driver's side wheel of a yellow school bus, the
German Shepherd that chased her into the street, barking, barking, barking, barking as if to resurrect her, to
make her play.

I thought I saw a bag of rags tossed into the street,
not Susie. The bundle lay still, not squirming.

"You kids stay here," Mom said, stumbling out the
patio door, worry affecting her tone. Neighbhors from
the block—the Freemans, Millers, Rusty and Inez Gill
(who had moved into Doc and Lillian's old house), Vera

Lauger, modest in a striped bathrobe, and Mrs. Flanagan, carting a weenie dog in her purse—had crowded onto the scene to investigate. I flattened the palm of my hands against my ears to bar a siren's scream.

The morning before, I had opened my eyes to see Susie hovering at the edge of my bed. She had tagged across the lawn with her mother who shared a pot of coffee with Mom. The ladies freshened cups of Folger's on the patio and Susie meandered upstairs to stir me from sleep with the brush of her breath. The bangs I had sheared when playing beauty shop sprouted above her pudgy face and timid eyes that stared me awake. She poked my cheek with curious, four-year-old fingers in the way she might nudge a shell with a stick, knowing a creature huddled inside.

"Soooo-zie. I'm still sleeeeep-ing," I said, a fake grump. She said nothing, preferring to listen than speak, protecting her lisp, the sssss sounds distorted by uncoordinated tongue and teeth. I let her crawl in beside me. One morning later, she lay pinned to the street. Framed by our picture window.

I had been the babysitter of choice in Heinrich's red-shingled bungalow since they moved there when Susie was two. Back then, I mashed her carrots, twined her fingers around a tipsy cup and afterwards, nested in Heinrich's living room, the carpet a minty green, the horsehair chair cradling us, the sound of my voice reciting Bo Peep until I tucked a listless Susie into her crib. It was a ritual, ours to keep.

Even then, when I was not yet twelve, I recognized my possessiveness. Saturday nights when the Heinrichs danced to a band at the Knights of Columbus Hall, I forced myself to stay awake, blinking sleep away, alert to Susie's slumbering turns in her bedroom—will she wake up? hungry or thirsty? afraid of the dark, dreaming?—until I heard their Pontiac pull into the drive after midnight, and Mr. Heinrich counted out cash in my hand, a whiff of whiskey on his breath.

"She was fine," I would tell them. "I read her to sleep."

That's the way we were, Susie and I, most of the time. The child, I felt, was mine; her custody, shared. I would never have let her fall in the street to be scraped up and carried away by ambulance, the wail of the siren, sickening.

129

"It's Susie," Mom said, confirming reality when she came back. "The dog scared her and she ran in front of the bus. The driver didn't see her."

"She can't be hurt, Mom," I begged, the threat of tragedy blurred by a mind unable to comprehend.

"I know. I know," Mom repeated, gathering me into her fullness, girdling me with firmness, reassuring me with her hold.

"They'll take care of her at the hospital," she said. I took her words as a promise.

It was September. The first day of my last year at St. Ellen's. Pencils had been ground into points, notebooks had been bought at the Ben Franklin, white laces were latticed through hand-me-down shoes, and the yard-and-a-half of cloth Mom bought at Robbin's Cotton Shop had been whipped into a pink polka dot skirt, the excess yardage pleated around my waist.

"I don't think there's anything we can do, except wait," Mom said. She sent me to school, polka-dotted and saddle-shoed, in the care of the eighth-grade nun, Sister Mary Domatilla. "You won't feel any better at home than you will at school," Mom reasoned.

Vincent had sanded and waxed four flights of hardwood floors during the summer, making the classroom smell like something old, polished and renewed. A glint of sun shined through raised windows and the air seemed clean, but a mix of urine and disinfectant in the boys' restroom overpowered the freshness by lunchtime. I didn't eat. During geography, Sister released the map of South America from a roller that looked like a window shade fastened to the top of the blackboard. She tapped the map's surface with her pointer as if to goad the country's silver mines into action by poking them, the way she would a lackluster student. Blotches of red, yellow and green, the only colors in a beige-painted classroom, separated regions on the map and stars marked major cities with scrabbled names, Paraguay, Uruguay and Venezuela. The shape of the country looked like a tornado, huge on top with a tail trailing.

Geography bored me, even more than science which came next. Sister scraped the pointer along the equator as if drawing the line herself.

"Get out your books. Page 64, Northern Hemisphere. Follow along," she said, reading aloud: "We are approaching the Autumnal Equinox, the time when day and night are equal. Soon, the darkness of winter—Winter Solstice—will come," she said. "The earth must sleep."

I felt confined by Sister's lessons. Trapped in the classroom, the hands of the wall clock measuring minutes, my mind associating the end of the school day with a finish line; crossing it, anxious and determined, I would go home to hear Mom say that Susie was fine, just fine, that Susie was grinning and standing, wiggling her toes. At ten to three, seconds before the last bell, Sister Superior tapped on the door. She spoke to Sister Domatilla in hushed confidence, their black habits bobbing in guarded conversation at the edge of the room. They beckoned to me, inviting me into the circle where Sister Domatilla whispered the news. Internal injuries.

"God had to take her," she said.

"No, God didn't!" I screamed, yowling, pummeling the nun with fists that had clenched automatically and churned like a dog paddling in lake water, desperate not to drown. I felt my knuckles slam the fleshy cushion between Sister's stomach and breasts. I hoped I hurt her.

"I hateyouhateyouhateyou!" I yelled, beating back the

truth with knotted fists, the whole class watching. Domatilla recoiled and Sister Superior lunged. She snatched me, blocking the spin of my fists, her thumbs and fingers cuffing my wrists, her force jerking me into the corridor to face her without witnesses. The power of Sister's clutch paralyzed and my chest hurt as if my heart had locked, too. I could not move and I would not cry. Because Sister was a liar.

"Look at me," she commanded, forcing me to stare into the tunnel of her nun's habit, its side partitions jutting out like horse blinders shielding distractions.

"Look at me! I want you to see me when I speak!" Sister said, *making* me hate her, *making* me look at the smoothness of her skin, whitened by convent life, and her eyes, dulled by piety, her lifeless expression neither cruel nor kind.

"You are a very passionate girl. That is a good thing," Sister said. "But you <u>must</u> <u>not</u> <u>hate</u>." She underlined words with controlled inflection. "And you <u>must</u> <u>not</u> strike anyone. Ever! Anger is a sin," she said, smothering my heartbreak, snuffing my terror, shaming agony away to smolder in a place where no words lived.

"Your mother is waiting for you in the foyer," Sister said. "She'll take you home. Pray for Susie's soul."

Our house was scented with spices after school. Mom had baked a tuna casserole and swirled powdered-sugar frosting over a pan of pecan rolls. Cinnamon colored the folds of rolled dough; it looked like art work, baked by the oven. Mom and Barb carried the offerings across the yard—the season of leaves, trees and golden zinnias almost over. Cars had parked at Heinrich's house, lining the side streets, not the road where Susie was hit. I saw the slow motion of neighbors, aunts and uncles, ladies from the church circle, Father Farrelly, and Mr. Heinrich's customers at the grain elevator, farmers in seed caps and overalls, ambling in and out of the house. I stopped watching, wondering how they could move through the rooms past the glazed eyes of Teddy Bears propped on blankets that smoothed Susie's bed. I pictured pieces of Mr. Potato Head scattered underfoot, our Mother Goose books stacked and unopened, Susie's sandals emptied in the closet, dresses dangling on hangers, limp as picked flowers in need of a drink. Mr. and Mrs. Heinrich should not look in that room as long as they live, I reasoned; if

Susie could never come home, how could they return to hear her stilled echo?

That was the day Susie died—she, a child, and I, a child myself. A dull, numbness followed me to bed that night in the kind of feeling I had begun to know, a moment cold, deep and unrelenting as the bottom of the lake at its darkest level, a moment that held hope under until it drowned, heavy, mossy, unable to float toward the sunshine of the surface. Mom sat on the edge of the bed to tuck me in when she and Dad came home from praying the rosary at visitation. The mattress sagged beneath her weight and Cookie made a lump under the sheet, stuffing herself into a hollow at my side, her warmth like grandma's hot water bottle pressed against my ribs.

"Take these," Mom said, shaking two adult-strength aspirin into my hand and offering a cup of water filled from the bathroom faucet. "Turn over. I'll rub your back."

She raised my pajama top to bare my skin and her hands began to play the base of my neck. I felt the pads of her fingers sweep across the ridge of my shoulders as if she had made a keyboard of me. She pressed her fingertips, hard and slow, adagio, up and down the sway of my spine, each ivory-hard nugget defined by her fingers on my flesh. I numbered my own bones as she touched them.

"I know how sad you are," Mom said, naming the grief that I had refused to claim.

"I'm not goin' to school tomorrow," I answered. In revolt, I would accept no comfort from Sister's prayerful vigil. It was prayer—wasn't it?—that had betrayed. It was prayer—wasn't it?—that played like an orchestra in the ears of the death angels as they passed through un-guarded gates to crush an innocent with a wheel while we breakfasted on oatmeal. No one stopped their mur-derous way, not Doc, not the nuns, not Mr. and Mrs. Heinrich, not me.

"I'll sit here with you for awhile," Mom promised, her fingers trailing. "See if you can get some sleep. Tomorrow's always a new day."

I saw Susie again, not in her closed coffin but through the veil of sleep. She woke me once more from slumber. I was babysitting her in a dream and she had fallen from her bicycle into the street. Training wheels tipped and spun, then stopped in the air as she laid on soiled pavement. I stood above Susie, giant-like, frozen, staring at the scene, imprisoned in the nightmare. I did not stir, nor did she. The only movement was blood draining from Susie's skull as I watched, unable to react to the bloody pool that was not red, but purple, as it crept across cement, crawling toward me until it bled into the sole of my shoe. I stood over her body, looking down, not moving, not speaking, not screaming, my hands outspread as if in consecration, powerless. I could not take care of her. I could not stop the blood nor escape its evil flow. I felt my own blood stir, rush in my veins, and I abhorred the animal in me, the primal urge to bend and run my finger through the blood in the street and taste it on my tongue. I woke, wanting to puke my thoughts and feelings.

Cookie leaped up when I did. Barb shifted on her pillow and stayed asleep on the opposite side of the bed. Feeling cold, I uncovered my sister and wrapped myself in the quilt Grandma had patched together for the bed Barb and I shared. Mom had left the hall light on for me and I wandered down the dimly-lit stairs, gliding like a sleepwalker through a slumbering house, past the kitchen and out the screen door into the midnight chill. Cookie trotted along, her coat already full for the winter.

I felt lost in the private wilderness of the yard I knew by heart. Before, the world beneath the boughs of the weeping willow had made me safe, happy, as if harbored in the glow of a lampshade. Wanting such comfort, I nested under the tree, my tree, the tree Dad had dug up from our old house because I sobbed when we left it. Permission granted by the new home owners, Dad bound the willow's roots in a moist clump of dirt and a gunny sack. He hauled my willow home, her tender branches protruding from the trunk of the car, her dainty leaves clinging.

"Here's your tree," he said, transplanting it for me. "So you can quit your cryin.'"

There the willow flourished. Her leaves grew ever slender, wispy—her silhouette, graceful and full as a taffeta gown, a dominant beauty in summer, a sleeping beauty in autumn. Blanketed, I laid myself out on the sound-proof floor beneath the willow's branches that were silver-plated by the moon. The scent of matted grass smelled of winter coming. I felt clammy and abandoned, remindful of a tender Walleye I had seen dad gut, its skin and flesh preserved, its innards emptied. I stiffened against the ground, suffocated by a feeling of helplessness, needing to breathe, trying not to drown in unwanted thoughts of the unjust death that had come to the kingdom of childhood.

I believed Susie belonged to me because I loved her. I thought she was mine.

Then she disappeared, silent and unseen as a stone dropped to the bottom of a pond.

I had found her and could not keep her. All that was left was memory and the brush of her breath one morning before.

Dear Pete

Pete skidded into the empty seat beside me in Honors English. Ginger and I had arrived before the bell, two Catholic girls freed from St. Ellen's, dressed for the first day of public high school, looking like models from *Teen Magazine*, parochial-school plaid upgraded to straight skirts and matching cardigans. The room was crammed, sweaty with public school boys, most of them muscled from farm work. And there wasn't a nun in sight. I passed a note to Ginger, ranking the boys in order of cuteness based on their hair, their lips, and the width of their shoulders.

Pete flashed a grin at me, though he hadn't made my list. By the second week, Dr. Martz, the English teacher who doubled as school principal, matched me to Pete as a study partner.

"I'll pick ya up tonight," Pete said, Friday after school. "We'll study."

Pete had descended from three generations of Danes, bricklayers by day, recluses by night. His dad's practice was to loosen his belt and stretch out on the sofa to sleep after supper; Pete's practice was to ease out of the driveway in the family Oldsmobile as soon as his dad started to snore. That night, he wheeled up in front of my house and honked the horn on the fat-fendered Olds, a full-bodied beauty of metallic bronze. I hopped in, Pete behind the wheel, a learner's permit in his pocket. He peeled out and we tooled around town, radio blaring, engine idling at the stoplight on Main. Pete was stalled at five-feet-five, but his toes reached the pedals and the big Olds made him a big man.

We repeated laps around the courthouse, blasted the horn at kids we knew, raced to the five-mile corner and back, then loitered in a vinyl booth at Sass McNally's Cafe where we drank chocolate-cherry Cokes and Pete sucked ketchup off his French fries. Patient as Cookie, my house-broken puppy asleep in the kitchen at home, Pete waited with me, the lone Catholic in the crowd, as the hands of the clock clicked to midnight so I could order a hamburger on meatless Friday.

"What'dya wanna play?" he asked.

"Everly Brothers," I answered.

Pete plugged nickels into the slot on a tableside jukebox and the coins ka-lunked through the gears, settling on *All I Have to Do is Dream* from the Top Forty. After Sass McNally's, we returned the Olds to the gravel drive at Pete's house and, from there, he walked me home in a full, September moon. We wandered to the boat dock and stopped to sit on a flat rock and dream about who and what we would become after high school. My destiny was on the stage, Broadway. Pete imagined himself as a Merchant Marine at Annapolis. Our shoes and socks lay scattered in sand and water that had lost the warmth of summer washed across our toes. Pete snapped a branch over his knee and scrawled his name on the beach with the finger of a brittle stick and we exchanged the fruits of friendship, simple and small.

"Anytime you need a date, I'll take you to the dance," he pledged. "Count on me. But you hafta sit beside me in the car and let me put my arm around you so it'll look like you're my girlfriend," he said.

I worried about striking a bargain with a boy whose ardor exceeded his conquests.

"And you hafta kiss me on the lips when I take you home," he added, upping the ante.

"I really kind of like Artie," I said, coming clean, clarifying my intentions.

"He's after Mary Sorenson," Pete said.

True, I eyed Artie in class, in the halls and the library. In turn, I saw him eye Mary, the Lutheran minister's daughter, the smartest, most precocious girl in the class. She glided on confidence through school corridors as if riding a homecoming float, corrected teeth locked into a queenly-looking smile. I wanted to wipe the smile off her face. Lipstick, too. Instead, I smiled back, camouflaging a festering jealousy, clinging to Pete as a boyfriend, hoping for the long shot, holding on to the sure thing.

Still, promises were promises and, silhouetted against my house on Harrison Street, we faced off for the kiss. Moths fluttered and bumped in the night, confused by the glow of the porch light Dad left burning until the last teenager came home. To be taller and to align his mouth with mine, Pete stood on the bottom porch step and leaned, eyes tight, meeting me halfway. The first time we kissed, I willed my eyes open so I could see everything: his butch-waxed hair, yellow as corn silk; his scar, a semi-circle left next to his nose by a bout of Chicken Pox; his muscles, pumped from lifting bricks, flexing through his shirtsleeves; his breath, warm, and his sandpaper lips, brushing mine.

"There," I said.

Pete grinned like a carnivore with sharp, uneven teeth.

"There's your kiss. And that's all."

From then on, through all of high school, I dated Artie, off and on. He dated Mary Sorenson, off and on. Pete was steadfast, courting me the best way he knew, through books. He led me through the classics and I succumbed to their seduction as if the pages were lurid nightclubs where characters I could not imagine lurked—waiting, I thought, for me. At St. Ellen's, I had studied liturgy, stories of martyrdom, saints and salvation. In public school, I descended to the depths of the *Inferno*. Pete and I skulked in castle corridors with Henry VIII. We brawled in the streets of Venice. We admired the impertinence of Hermes in Greek mythology. We burrowed and wormed our way from the Renaissance through Goethe to the Romantics. I thrilled to Pete's Romeo and he applauded my Juliet. We fingered the lines of *Walden Pond* as if the words were Braille, then scribbled inspirations of our own.

Queen Clytaemnestra, wife of Agamemnon, mother of Orestes, obsessed me. *I'll call my daughter Clytaemnestra someday—though she'll hate me for it,* I promised myself. The splendor of her name, Clytaemnestra, her title, the tempo of her soliloquies, the resonance of her beauty, the allure of her deviousness disturbed my rhythm, interrupted my breath. She stirred inside me. Her power caught my throat, her crown weighed against my forehead, her gowns snaked around my legs, her jewels caressed my neck, her rings warmed my fingers. Imagining her disarmed me, though I knew not why.

In contrast, my relationship with Pete stayed oddly intimate and warm, though platonic, through the green and blue of summers, through the harvest's pumpkin color, and into winter's sterile white. Snow fell, almost always, before Thanksgiving. Nature then offered little escape from blasts of Canadian air. Ice-fishing shacks popped up, ugly as pimples on the surface of the lake. Winds whipped through a cloth coat and crawled under my collar when Ginger and I walked home from school, ice skates slung over our shoulders, stopping at the lake to etch out afternoons in the shape of figure eights.

Snowmobiles or Nash Ramblers with chains clamped to tires ploughed through two-foot drifts and took us where we wanted to go. For comfort, we congregated at basketball games, VFW dances, Boy and Girl Scouts, 4-H meetings, and church. We feasted on Maid Rites at the Corner Cafe, Walleye Pike at Friday night fish fries, and stacks of flapjacks at the Izaak Walton League's Winter Pancake Feast. As protectors of the lake's wildlife, fish, and fowl, the league raised funds by peddling pancakes and raffle tickets. For a buck a crack, folks bought a chance to win fifty by guessing the date when the ice would go out of the lake and release the '38 Dodge parked near Second Island, allowing it to plunge like a huge steel frog into the water, burbling and gurgling its way to the bottom. For Pete and me, the jalopy was an ice palace before it went down.

The last Christmas Eve we spent together, we warmed to the orange and blue burn of logs in the fireplace, the house quiet as a library after everyone in my family, except Grandpa McCarty (a widower then) had gone to Midnight Mass. We slurped cups of hot chocolate and licked the scorch off melted marshmallows, waiting for Grandpa to fall asleep in his easy chair while he sifted through sports scores in the newspaper. Soon enough, Grandpa's eyelids fluttered, his head flopped, and his pipe dropped to his chest. Pete picked the pipe up and brushed embers from Grandpa's Pendleton so he wouldn't catch himself and the house on fire. Then we pulled stocking caps over our ears and waded out into the pure snow of Christmas morning. We turned our backs on the bite of the wind and waded through snowdrifts that showed no other footprints, finding our way to the banged-up jalopy parked on the lake. Cold tingled my cheeks as if they had been stung. Using a jackknife from his pocket, Pete chipped the frozen seal from the driver's side and forced the door to creak open. Ice split and shattered into shards as it gave up its grip. We wedged in behind the front seat, huddling in the back, lighting matches and puffing illicitly on Pall Malls bought at the all-night Conoco. Our breath, visible in the cold, jetted out before us like a persistent ghost taking firm shape in the fog of cigarette smoke. A pattern of frost as fine as lace on the edges of Grandma's handkerchiefs prettied the car windows. Pete pulled off a mitten and wrote on the icy glass with the heat of his exposed finger—MM + PS—though frost filled the initials in immediately, obscuring the letters, washing them away like water erases a message in the sand. Instead of exchanging Christmas gifts, we exchanged little kisses, experimentally. The temperature had already plunged to below zero that late in the evening, that late in the year. In the alchemy of our friendship, the tint of the moon turned to a silver stream through crystal windows. We didn't feel cold in our cocoon.

By the time Pete graduated Valedictorian, the Trojan he had hidden in his wallet was smashed flat, its wrapper crisp and dried, rendered useless by time and circumstances. It was, in a way, like his football uniform, something for show. Each season, he had suited up for the squad, but rarely got in the game. Eventually, as eager graduates, we left Emmetsburg in the way a train departs from a station, slowly, lurching at first, then full steam ahead to some other world, to destinations unknown. I left Pete and looked not behind, but forward, a curious passenger witnessing the world as I passed by.

"You guys set up the tree," I said, addressing my husband and sons so many Christmases, so many years, so many miles down the track. "I'll find the ornaments."

I rooted through basement storage shelves in disarray: summer clothes and sandals and a blue velvet box that hoarded notes, charms, old pictures and saved letters. One, long forgotten, had been penned in blue ink on a nice parchment. It was a letter from Pete, the only one he ever sent. He had tracked me down, found my address, and wrote in fire light from the hearth that he, a mason, had built of stone.

"*Since I last saw you, I graduated with a B.S. in psychology from Iowa U. and went for an MFA in creative writing, working some with Kurt Vonnegut,*" he wrote.

"*Finishing at Iowa, I tried teaching English at a community college. I disliked the experience and removed myself. After that, I worked in a steel mill for a while and, having married a girl who wanted to leave the Midwest, I soon wound up in New Hampshire. Along the way, I somehow got two children—a girl and a boy—then lost them in a divorce. The children live in Provo, Utah, with their mother and I fly them back and forth in summer for six-week visits. It's a shock to be a family man, then not, then again, but we all try to adjust and it works out okay considering.*

After my divorce, I lived and worked on Cape Cod for a while, where I hung around the waterfront and found that being a single man wasn't so bad after all. Soon I returned to N.H., got involved with a lovely woman who turned out to be a fugitive from the FBI. We had many fine adventures, including hitchhiking to Mexico in midwinter, exploring the Sierra Madre with a French filmmaker named Jean-Paul, and almost getting busted by the Federales which would have put us in gruesome jails forever. But we lucked out.

I laughed, though there was no one there to hear me. Pete, almost busted, had lucked out. Was his story fact or fiction? I did not know and it did not matter. I imagined Pete as he might have imagined entertaining me, his letter like a book in my hand, the story he created for me unfolding, one page at a time.

Later, I took up with a singer who traveled up and down the East Coast with her band, name of Purly Gates of Purly and the Waste Band, he continued.

We're still together, living in Acworth, N.H., in my little house in the woods. When she's not singing, we toast our feet in front of my fine fireplace and raise lots of vegetables, but not as much hell as we used to.

So far, I've avoided tying the knot again. The prospect of marriage scares me a little, but Purly and I are pretty settled in anyway, and she takes good care of my kids in summer. The winter before last, Purly got a job singing in the Lost Resort on an island near Tortola, British Virgin Islands, where we lived on our own houseboat. The only way to get there was by boat, so all day long..."

Pete's letter ended there because the last page had been lost, sacrificed to the years, as he had been. I had wondered—though rarely—what might have happened to Pete and Purly and the kids they shared in the summer, but the letter I wrote in response to his came back to my mailbox, unopened. Addressee unknown.

You found me!, my letter, though unopened, would have told him. *I'm not on Broadway. I'm here, in a bungalow in Kansas City, St. Peter's parish, nurturing a husband and two sons, a dog and a turtle, living scenes from a script written not by me, but by the conventions of society. I have been cast; I play the part.*

Pete, I had confessed, *no one before you or since has shown me a greater love of literature, nor greater loyalty. Had I not been so young, Pete, I might have placed a higher premium on the qualities of friendship, rather than taking such a prize for granted.*

It was not that I longed for lost moments Pete and I had written in the sands of childhood. It was that, as an adult, I felt a wisp of shame, a sense that I had been a disappointment. To Pete and to myself. Because there had been no bitterness with Pete, did I not taste the sweet? Had I inherited my father's emphasis on wealth and the unattainable, I wondered. Had pettiness fed a girl's inability to value that which had cost little? The pretense of a date and a kiss on the lips in the porch light is all Pete had asked of me.

His dad and Blondie, his bridge-playing, substitute-teaching mother were dead, I had heard, and I didn't know where to find their son. Busy with life, I hadn't actually tried.

I bound the letters together, Pete's ribboned to mine, his last page missing. I tucked them into the velvet box, returning them to storage, then stood on a stool—Christmas was coming!—to search top shelves, looking for ornaments, hoping none, especially the most delicate, had been broken.

Prairie Home

Mom and Dad deposited me in Berry Hall with Susie, my roomie, a girl who sewed her own clothes and stitched needlepoint to calm her nerves. They wished us well and drove out of town. I watched them make a getaway, stranding me there.

"It won't be that long. Thanksgiving's just around the corner," Mom said when she left. "You'll love it here. When you make up your mind that you want to."

Through an uncurtained window, I surveyed the landscape of my future at a state college in Nebraska. The prairie grounds looked prematurely withered, like November rather than September, like an ending rather than a start. It was no secret I wanted to go to Iowa U, that campus buzzing with intellectual energy, that commons blazing with orange and red Maples; I remembered it that way from Jerry's hospital stay when we were kids. Instead, I was sentenced to confinement in Berry Hall, a room plain and bare except for a four-drawer desk and Susie sitting on a bed with brush rollers in her hair. Her middle finger was thimbled and she stitched a hem by hand. I felt like bolting, running free. But my luggage blocked the door.

McBurney was to blame. My academic advisor for senior year, McBurney had summoned me and I had answered, tapping my knuckles on a half-opened door and stepping into an office putrid with the odor of his coffee and pipe tobacco.

"You wanted to see me?" I said.

"Sit."

He didn't look up.

I slid into a hard side-chair, its seat broader than mine. I pressed my shoulders against the back slats and squeezed my buttocks together to hold myself erect, properly quiet and still, waiting diminutively for him to speak. A nameplate spelled *Dr. McBurney Allison* in white Helvetica on a green plastic strip. McBurney was head of the English department, the Ph.D. granting him greater supremacy than I felt he deserved. A large, bulky man, a Scot, he rooted through stacks of books and papers, tests and student essays that had spilt out of folders scattered on the fortress of his desk, ignoring me in his search.

I waited, counting the number of dust rolls curled at the feet of bookshelves McBurney had shoved against the walls of his den, a room in the back of the building. Twin windows above his desk shaped sunlight into streams and I watched dust particles swim in the beams as a diversion, as a way to divert my eyes and avoid looking at twisted hairs, dark sprouts, that crept over his shirt collar and crawled out of the cavities of his nose and ears. Hair patched his head like an unmanaged garden. He was a hairy beast, a mammoth, one that I normally encountered as he slouched through the halls in tweed, an elbow-patched jacket tainted with the musk of tobacco smoke. He would study the floor, holding his head down as he ushered himself through the corridors. In class, his jacket hitched up in the back and exposed slack pants when he chalked assignments on the board. That day, seeing him in his confines was a necessity. He had sent for me, as if he had a matter to settle.

"Are you prepared for this discussion?" he asked, without looking up.

I felt invisible in the face of his authority, in his refusal to acknowledge me with his eyes.

"I think so," I said. "I'm pretty sure I'm going to take that scholarship at Iowa. In theater."

"You want to be *stage struck* the rest of your life?" he bellowed, slamming a hand on his desk. He stared at me then, leaning across the desk, zeroing in on my face.

"You think you're going to be an *actress?*" He sneered, pelting me with contempt. "A *staaaaar?*"

"Not a star...," I said, grasping at denial, the sole, flimsy defense that surfaced.

"You think you can live on *ah-plaaaaause?*" he asked, interrupting me before I could think. "One day, you'll be have to live in the r*eal* world."

Until then, I had pitied him. Rumors had hissed around town, saying his wife was crazy. Saying they had buried an infant child before they had come here. Saying she hibernated in their rental house across the street from the high school, taking to her bed, a psychological invalid, like tragic women I had read about in romance novels.

He reminded me of the captain of the Atlantic Queen,

160

a whaling ship trapped by crushing ice in *Ile*, the one-act we had entered in state competition. I played the captain's emotionally fragile wife, doomed to a watery grave with captain and crew of the stranded ship. Tension on stage heightened as the echo of a fog horn synchronized with the wife's cries and terror plunged her into madness. I manipulated the audience in that final scene, breathing life into O'Neill's lines, finding exhilaration in the silence before a rush of applause, as if I were a mother in the breathless second after giving birth, awaiting the sound of a newborn's cry. Was it a level of omnipotence I felt? Was it cathartic release? Was it spiritual, a reverence for the glory of literature's beauty and depth, immeasurable as the sea? Or was it being with the boys in the cast?

Mrs. Dinges, the drama coach, had rewarded me with the lead role after cheering my performances in Saroyan, Chekhov and Tennessee Williams. The bonus was that she had recruited lanky basketball players for the stage in their off-season; they swaggered through the script in high-buckled boots, navy pea coats, stocking caps and ratty fake beards. Russell crossed his eyes to add a nuance to his shipmate's character and then, crazed from hacking ice with an ax, stumbled melodramatically on stage to warn the captain of mutiny. John Hall, Captain Keeney, pinched his hat in his hand and implored God to favor man over nature, to spare his crew and save his wife from a descent into darkness. As the captain's frail wife, I fluttered like a captive bird on stage, boney shoulder blades poking the back of my costume. The picture of the cast on the front page of the school newspaper captured me, flirtatiously out of character, surrounded by basketball boys, poseurs in pasted-on beards. Costumed in a high-necked Victorian dress, I wore a smile, gloating in an enviable configuration, the only girl in a cast of ten men.

There were moments in *Ile*, powerful ones, that brought me the Helen Hayes Award and a bounty of scholarship dollars. Applause had nourished conceit and I had swept into McBurney's office on a feeling of guilelessness. I hadn't expected to be booed, to feel dishonored, to flinch as McBurney slashed my dreams with words he hurled like carving knives.

"Earn a degree in elementary education. You can get certified to teach with sixty credits," he said. "That's appropriate for a woman. And kiddies need good teachers."

I felt myself deflate, no longer special, no longer divine. The feelings I had come with, confidence and arrogance, gone. McBurney dismissed my ambition and then dismissed me, sending me slinking back to class, like a pup that had been batted with a newspaper. In less than ten minutes, any tinge of compassion I had felt for one whose wife was strangely disturbed had darkened into contempt. He said he would write a letter of recommendation for my application to teacher's college; that made me hate the man of education who would forge his name on the documents of my future.

"McBurney's right," Dad said at home that night. Dad heard my complaint from behind the newspaper, distancing himself in the usual way. He peered over the evening edition as he issued his decree, making his decision seem all the more black and white, final as the day's news.

"Get a teacher's certificate," he said, as if he and McBurney had conspired. "You'll have that to fall back on if something happens to your husband someday. A teacher can earn almost four-thousand dollars a year. And get summers off."

I made a plea to change his mind, but to Dad, marching his daughter down the path of sensibility was not punishment; it was security. My pursuits, he said, had been a little fanciful, fine for high school, unrealistic for life.

"You can go where your brother goes," Dad said, closing the case. "He'll look out for you."

I cried into the night and for days after, sniveled in my pillow. I cried—and who cared?

"Why don't you stick up for yourself, instead of whining all the time," Barb asked, challenging my right to claim a dream if I lacked the courage to defend it.

I felt in mourning, saddened by the loss of fictional lives I had loved in plays and books. I had walked onstage in their image, disguised myself in their clothes, and released their feelings, making them mine. All along, I supposed, I had lurked in made-up stories, a pretender, bartering her life for applause and admiration. Dad and McBurney saw my tendencies as starry-eyed, lacking in market value and, in time, I acquiesced. I exchanged the person I had hoped to become for the daughter Dad expected me to be.

By then, Ginger had packed her bags for Stephen's, a girls' school in the South. Pete was headed to the University of Iowa. Mary Sorenson enrolled in the church college of her father's choosing. Artie had not announced a decision, if he had made one. And soon, my new address was Berry Hall where Susie and I shared a desk, a closet and not a single interest.

Designed as a residence for men, Berry Hall had converted to co-ed to ease housing shortages. I, along with the other girls of Berry Hall, innovated. We feathered our nests, storming through five floors in the east wing, thumb-tacking Elivs posters to bedroom walls, dressing naked windows in tie-back sheers, and converting men's urinals to flower pots in the bathrooms. A central foyer with a wood-burning fireplace stood as an easily maneuverable passage between the girls and amorous boys who lurked in the opposite wing. Thus, the Berry Hall tradition: the sound of giggles, soft as the tinkle of piano music, drifting from behind closed doors as girls hosted visitors after curfew.

The calendar had flipped to the 1960s. By then, the word liberation fit into every coed's vocabulary and a packet of birth control pills fit into every purse. Molly Molloy, a girl down the hall, got pregnant despite the pill and while we teetered on the cusp of a revolution, she was banished to a home for unwed mothers, cloistered in secrecy. Her friends and relatives were told that Molly had gone to study abroad; fooling no one, she was to reappear months later, unscarred and renewed. Skipping Mass one Sunday, I borrowed Paul Pak's pickup, the Chevy truck he used to haul me on dates after hauling horses at his daddy's ranch. I drove alone to visit the girl they called Mary at the convent in Sioux City. The nuns led me to Molly's room where we strained to be pleasant, pretending everything would be okay, though she would never see the baby, nor be allowed to touch the child that would be adopted away. Molly's mother was dead and her father, rigidly Catholic, disowned her, she said. She crossed her swollen legs at the ankles, primly, posing on the edge of a cot, one among dozens of narrow beds lined against a wall in an open room that smelled like Lysol. I felt nauseous as I watched the cotton smock rise and fall over her bloated belly with her every breath.

I left, feeling sad for Molly, not knowing what to do,

except keep her secret. I worried how the pregnant girl, a social outcast, would find her way as the broken line of her family extended to a third generation—her mother dead, her father estranged, her friends fickle, and her baby to be cast away like a too-small fish, the legacy of love disintegrated. I felt haunted by the look on Molly's face, blank as the orphanage walls, neither she nor her baby belonging to anyone. I tried not to think about the repugnance of Molly's fate or the unwanted child she had signed away; there was nothing I could do but put her circumstances behind like the miles that lay between, abandoning her in the way she would abandon the baby.

Traveling narrow dirt roads on the way back to campus, I cut through the countryside, its color drained after harvest, and I wondered—what would my father do if I shamed him? I pushed thoughts of Molly out of my mind, thinking instead about Paul, remembering when we met; seeing Paul for the first time was like spotting a stallion, the grandest animal on campus. Knowing his own beauty, he tipped his Stetson, uncovering Rock-Hudson-hair when he flirted, his eyes the color of his truck, baby blue. At six-feet-two, his stride took on the look of a swagger. Soon, though, I recognized that Paul's view of the future was uncomplicated, as simple as his mind.

"I'm gonna get an education, marry me a college girl, and father six kids," he said, proud as if he was already handing out cigars. "I'll have my own Six Pak!" he announced, saddlng his manhood with his plan for procreation. Paul held me in his sights as one he wished to make his bride and cart home in his pickup truck, fencing me in like one of the ponies on his ranch in Ponca City.

"Not me, Paul. You'd better get another girl," I said. My new lust for independence mushroomed when it clashed with his ideas. "I'm not having six babies. And you can't fence me in. "

Remembering Molly, I knew that Paul Pak would not make an unwed mother or a married mother of me. Yet we ambled on, meeting for Maid Rites in the cafeteria, falling into the easy gait of friendship. By then, Susie had sewn floral pillows to toss on the beds to make our dorm room homey. Berry Hall girls flocked to our quarters on cold, prairie nights, toasted themselves under my electric blanket and listened to me read Mom's letters aloud:

Your daddy got home about 5:30 and I had pork chops and gravy browning on the stove, she wrote. *I mashed a batch of garlic potatoes and opened a jar of kernel corn your grandma canned last summer. Delish! Carrie Miller stopped by with a cherry cobbler. Carrie loves to bake (because she loves to eat!). I warmed the cobbler and Dad had a little vanilla ice cream with his. Hope you're doing fine, honey. I'm sure you're getting smarter every day.—Love, your mom and dad*

Slitting the envelope on Mom's letters felt like opening an oven door and releasing the freshness of her words. In general, I had settled in, emboldened by academic choices I made second semester. I had defected from the school of education, cutting classes, surprising myself with the satisfaction I found in defiance. Tip-toeing out of lecture halls, responding to the lure of open auditions in the theater felt so right that I didn't see it as wrong. Evenings, I shut myself up after curfew and wrote plays and essays, feeling the headiness of my true loves—reading, writing, and play acting. I hid my decision from Mom and Dad, and escaping my brother's watch was easy. We inhabited the same campus and crossed the same quadrangle, but navigated different waters. Dickie (Richard at college) scrimmaged on the football field; I auditioned for parts and rehearsed on a paint-splattered set. He was an icon, captain of the football team; I was popular with cheerleaders because I was his sister. He lugged his books to a job as night manager at the Sinclair station while earning his business degree; I had all but abandoned study. He found little time to monitor his sister since he was a senior and I was a freshman, a speck on the wall.

Cast in a round of plays, theatre people became my groupies. I landed a lead in JB and Dr. Rogers, department chair, recruited me to read Edna St. Vincent Millay's *Ballad of the Harp Weaver* for a television special taped at an ABC affiliate in Norfolk. Star-struck and feeling giddy from the privilege, I rouged my cheeks in the dressing room mirror the day of the taping. I slicked my lips with cherry-flavored gloss and primped for an on-camera debut, appraising my image in the dressing room mirror, marveling that, with small bones and a natural spray of Irish-red hair, I resembled the lady poet.

Extra rouge! I decided, though the show aired in black and white. I swirled a brush in a pot of Max Factor and swabbed each cheek with crimson. Behind me, the door to the dressing room opened and I saw Dr. Rogers reflected in the mirror. She entered the dressing room, clicking the latch and moving toward me in thick-soled shoes, her hands buried in pockets of the brown cardigan that was her rehearsal costume, fingering Kleenex and crumpled, scribbled notes she'd sometimes pull out of her pockets to read. She slipped bifocals off her nose and let them dangle from a string around her neck to flop against soft bulges, her breasts.

"Let's look at your hair," she said, standing close.

She had the smell of licorice on her breath. Taller than me, taller than most everyone, she peered down, sharp-eyed. Our reflection, duplicated in the mirror made it seem as if there were four of us instead of two, doubling the impact of a broad-boned woman, plain as a work horse. She must have been sixty, old as my grandmother, I thought. My shoulders felt heavy under the unwelcome attention. I looked away, focusing on pages of the book spread open on the vanity. She smoothed my shoulder with one hand, touching me in the way an expectant woman strokes her stomach's contents. In her right hand, she raised my chin as if lifting a baby bird, her palm as the nest. She leaned closer, too close, and tilted my face, examining it in the artificial light.

"Your hair's pretty," she said. "But it will shadow your face on camera. We can't have that."

She touched the padded part of her fingers to my forehead and moved her hand across my brow in slow motion. She swept my hair up, held it, finger tips lingering on my forehead, then she let the hair flow and drop. I flinched.

"Your features are so delicate," she said. "Such a tiny face. The perfect Nora."

I pressed my fingers along the seam of open pages and buried my bookmark among poems that waited to be read. I clapped the book shut, picked it up, and held it like a shield against my chest.

"Come by my house this weekend," Dr. Rogers said. I looked up to see her scrawl on a scrap of paper she pulled from her pocket. "I'm on the north side of the square," she said, handing me her telephone number and address. "We'll read lines from *A Doll's House*."

She left me with a feeling of queasiness, as disappointed as if she had taken something from me, though she had not. She had given. And she hinted at more. Confused by my emotions—uncertainty, a sense of revulsion, apprehension and, underlying it all, the feeling that I had been *chosen.*

I procrastinated, postponing my response for a week. I was afraid to offend although in a peculiar, indefinable way, I felt offended.

Near dusk one evening, feeling an obligation to respond—she was, after all, department chair—I stuffed the scrap of paper in my pocket and cut around the block on my way to the book store. I passed rows of homes in Dr. Rogers' neighborhood until one house matched the number she had written. I stopped in front and kicked through leaves that, wet from an evening rain, littered the sidewalk and stuck to the soles of my sneakers. Books, some bleached by the sun, lay sprawled on the front seat of a faded gray Plymouth parked in the drive. Window shades on the house were drawn, closed to the world like a dead person's eyes. She had lived in the house, her mother's only companion, until the old woman had died. I imagined a living room, a sunless parlor, furnished in damask sofa and matching chairs, brittled by plastic coverings. On a bureau, candy would be coagulated, its sugar turned to gel, stuck to the bottom of the dish. Cat hair would be hidden in rugs, flying like dander if someone walked through the room. I hesitated on the edge of the lawn, drawn there by curiosity, immobilized by uncertainty. I didn't *want* to be teacher's pet, the department chair's special friend. But I wanted to be Nora.

I crouched on the sidewalk, one knee in the leaves, pretending to tie my shoe, to stall, until night replaced day and crows flocked to the trees at the edge of the property, filling the branches like raucous black leaves. A chill seeped in through the sleeves of my jacket and felt like cold rain. A porch light flicked on and, not wanting to be detected, I stood up and ran, shivering. When I reached the courthouse, I followed a line of street lamps across cobbled stones on the square, past the Lost Sock Laundromat and the Burger Joint, down an incline to a stone wall that surrounded a pond, stopping off at the student union, warming myself with sips of hot chocolate while waiting for a three-cheese pizza I carried back to the dorm. Susie was sewing when I got home, hemming a skirt, inching it up so the shape of her legs would please her boyfriend, Alex, a quarterback on the football team.

I dropped a dime into the hall pay phone. I dialed Dr. Rogers' number and held my breath as the rings pulsed in my ear.

"Hello?"

"Dr. Rogers?" I asked, trying to hold my voice steady.

"This is Eleanor," she said. From the listlessness in her voice, it was impossible to tell if she was angry or sad or old.

"This is Martha McCarty, Dr. Rogers. I won't be able to come by your house to read lines," I said, assaulting her vanity, rejecting tradeoffs, gratuities that may have been secretly exchanged.

I felt strong after the call. I felt strong again when I read for Nora during open auditions. Once-banned and controversial, Ibsen's tragedy in which Nora shuns convention and abandons all she has known, courageously choosing freedom and passing through a door to new possibilities, affected me. I felt the message personally. I chose the final scene for auditions: tense exchanges that led Nora to emancipation, to the point where she took her place at the door, ready to depart, the symbol of freedom, her suitcase, in her hand:

I have no idea what will become of me, I read instinctively, understanding Ibsen, understanding Nora, better than I understood myself...*at any rate, I release you from all duties. You must not feel yourself bound, any more than I shall. There must be perfect freedom on both sides.*

I read with conviction, outshining other hopefuls.

Two days after auditions, Dr. Rogers posted the cast list near the box office. No call backs. The show had been cast. Across from the lead role—NORA—appeared the name NOREEN LONG. I scanned the list, role by role in descending order, and found my name printed at the bottom of the announcement under STAGE CREW.

For the run of the show, I lurked in the wings, disheartened by watching Noreen take Nora's bows in the nourishing footlights. Back at Berry Hall, second semester grades, the marks of my folly, clogged my mailbox from a mix of core requirements and education classes I had skipped. Cs, Ds, Fs. One A, in Oral Interp. As a member of the crew, I swept the stage with an industrial-sized broom, cleaning up, pushing rose petals that had fallen from Noreen's bouquets, helping strike the set after the cast's final bows. I declined an invitation to the cast party after the last matinee. Paul found me sitting alone in the darkened theater when everyone had gone. I longed to go home.

"I'll cheer you up," he said. He led me to the parking lot, opened the passenger-side door and waited while I slid in. We drove to Norfolk for a movie, *The Children's Hour*. Shirley MacLaine played my namesake, Martha, a schoolmistress. The light in Martha's eyes extinguished once her career was threatened by the taint of scandal: an accusing student whispered a claim that Martha shared an inordinate affection with a woman, an illicit relationship forbidden by propriety. The movie's themes of malice and cancerous suspicion sobered me since, again, I saw a reflection of my soul in the body of fiction. I realized I could have been cast as the venomous student who was capable of poisoning Dr. Rogers' reputation. In truth, she, a tenured department chair, had not compromised me, a failing student, except in my imagination. It was the stirrings of instinct, not fact, that had

177

prompted unsubstantiated suspicions in my mind. Dr. Rogers was guilty of wielding the balance of power, lifting the curtain on the society of politics I had only begun to experience.

On the drive home, Paul plopped his Stetson, a hat the color of dried bones, in the middle seat, but it was silence, not Paul's hat, that separated us. Except for the rattle of the truck's fenders and the hum of the engine under the hood, the atmosphere felt funereal, as if our friendship was doomed. I used the solitude to sort through thoughts, searching for interpretation, wishing to understand all that affected me.

Rain rinsed the windshield and bathed the air, making it smell clean. Patsy Cline wailed *I'm crazy, crazy for feelin' so blue* on a country station.

"You've been a good friend, Paul," I said.

"What's goin' on with you," he asked, Patsy Cline singing *Crazy for lovin' you.*

That night, miles from all cathedrals, I felt I had found a new faith, not in the Church, not in my father, not in a husband on a ranch, but in the being that dwelled in me and had nearly suffocated. A feeling I could neither name nor explain to my cowboy companion altered me while we rattled down the road. A sense of desolation receded like the rain and in the same instant, newness flooded in. Tears sprang from wherever they had hidden, undammed by a force that was not intellectual, but instinctual. I felt a sensation of release, facing loss while harboring hope.

Paul pulled into the A&W automatically as if his truck operated by remote.

"I think I'll have choc'late," he said, contemplating a malt. "I had strawberry yesterday. Maybe I'll try choc'late-strawberry," he said, plumbing the depths of his philosophical explorations. Afterwards, we were one more couple among the clusters lingering on the steps of Berry Hall until curfew.

"How about Saturday night?" Paul asked. "Wanna do somethin'?"

"I wish I could," I lied. I had no idea what my future included, though I knew it did not include him.

I shook Susie awake when I went in, making her the audience for my midnight revelation.

"I'm leaving school," I said. "And I won't be back."

"You can't leave," Susie whined. "It's mid-semester.

Who'll live with me?" Sleep had changed the shape of her eyes from round to slatted.

"You'll be fine," I said, as if my mom were talking, promising the best, concealing the worst. I snatched skirts out of the closet and started to pack.

The next morning, with no place to go, I was Nora, suitcase in hand. I boarded a Trailways bus, destined to face my father who hadn't yet seen my grades. He had called the week before to say he had gone, not happily, to Iowa Trust and Savings to cover a forty-five dollar overdraft in my college account, a fortune in student's wages. I was bankrupt and flunking out of college, but feeling free. The bus pulled away from the station, gliding easily as a steamer on a stream, rolling mile after nautical mile as I, a prairie-school fugitive, sailed away.

Editors, Hated and Revered

Walt's pipe scented his office with cherry-blend smoke that wrapped wisps around the bare knob of his head. I stood, immobile as stone, eyes tilted downward in remorse and embarrassment.

"Have a seat," he said, nodding toward an empty chair.

He sat, too, and there was a face-off with the expanse of his desk as a dividing line. At no other time did I remember feeling so small, so physically shrunken, as if I were a six-year-old who had gone to see the Wizard. Walt's rigid, tall-shouldered posture, his omnipotence as managing editor combined with his cryptic tone, were reasons to be intimidated. Walt was not known to raise his voice, nor was he one to be caught smiling.

He gripped the bowl of his pipe in his left palm, his fingers supporting it like a truss. He clamped the stem between his teeth, making bite marks on it. With his right hand, he flattened the tobacco with a tamper, packing it tight, like garden soil pressed by the toe of a tiny shoe. Sheets of glass partitioned Walt's office and smoke spiraled over the walls and stretched itself invisibly thin, leaving only its trace, a whiff in the air.

I felt locked in an isolation booth, though beyond the glass panels I heard the sound box of the newsroom—an exotic hum like music vibrating from stringed instruments, the blend of voices forming a chorus, phones jingling as if Tinkerbell floated in the room. Beneath it all, the *clicketyclicketyclack* of AP wire machines issuing this-just-in stories and photos. Fingers drummed keys of Royal typewriters for percussion and the sweet *ping!* of carriage returns punctuated the end of each line of copy. The City Room was open with no partitions, except for Walt's. Everyone worked at metal desks in a wide-open space.

"What happened?" Walt asked. He wanted facts.

He propped his pipe in the ashtray on his desk, smoke signals rising. He flipped to a blank page in a reporter's notebook and fixed his gaze on me, making me feel frozen. Behind my back, I felt other eyes. Through the glass walls of Walt's cubicle, I knew reporters were watching me squirm in the chair, loving a good story.

I had slapped Jay, the Farm Editor, and knocked him out of his chair in the newsroom. That was the story.

I had sent Jay reeling, falling flat on his back, the spindles of his arms and legs sprawling on the floor in a room packed with witnesses, sportswriters, proofreaders, photographers, and other editors, including Society. Jay rose from the mat like a fallen boxer, his hand clenched in a white-knuckled fist, his right arm pulled back, ready to spring. A couple of sportswriters had leaped into action, grabbing Jay and pinning him like a jailbird, arms behind his back, restraining him so he couldn't hit me.

"I'd really rather not talk about it," I said.

Walt had missed the incident while downstairs in the press room. I was reluctant to give him details since he was the one who had hired me and I didn't want him to regret it. How I had wormed my way into Walt's world at *The Messenger* was a story within a story, as implausible or wondrous as any.

"Walt," said the angel-lady at the employment agency

when she had called his office the year before. She knew Walt from Fort Dodge Emmanuel Lutheran where he served as a church elder who passed the collection plate and served communion in his brown Sunday suit (brown shoes, too).

"I think I have just the person you're looking for," the woman had said, pitching me onto the auction block, endorsing me, a college drop out whose parents, their tolerance exhausted, forced an end to my sorry melodrama, a script I had written and starred in myself.

"Here are the keys to the car," Mom had said, dangling them in my face. "Fix your hair. Put on some lipstick. And go find a job."

It was August, the dog days. Double windows in the employment office had ushered sunlight in to drench the rooms in suffocating heat. A fan atop a file cabinet oscillated, blowing its hot breath on me. I wilted while waiting for the woman to sell me like a used car. A perfect-looking chassis coming off the assembly line—secretly, a lemon.

I felt clammy in panty hose and a seersucker suit. Arrid Cream turned to paste in my armpits, my arms glued to my sides.

"She has a *smattering* of college," the woman went on, trying to pass me off as legit. "And a little on-the-job experience."

Interpreted, experience constituted one summer I had worked at the Emmetsburg paper, writing social notes:

"*Mrs. Gib Knutsen hosted the Monday morning Bridge Club at the Knutsen home on State Street. Guests enjoyed shortcake topped with whipped cream and strawberries picked fresh from the family garden. We asked Mrs. Knutsen to share her shortcake recipe...*"

"She's strong in English and literature," she continued. The woman was either a marketing genius or an untrustworthy liar. I had started to believe her myself.

She arranged a meeting at *The Messenger*, Walt's province. He set a chair at an empty desk and laid out a pencil with a pink rubber eraser alongside a stack of exams, reams of grammar, writing and proofreading exercises. After the tests, Walt interrogated me in an afternoon-long interview, then led me through the plant, including a tour of the press room, a dingy, oily-smelling underground where men in aprons and dungarees, ink-stained faces as black as coal miners, rolled their sleeves above their elbows and crawled, mite-like, into the machinery, tinkering with the presses before an evening edition.

Less than a week had passed when Walt's call came through to me. I hung up the phone and jumped into a jerky dance in Mom and Dad's kitchen after Walt telephoned to seal a deal. He had critiqued my writing samples and polled my references, extracted a glowing report from the high school superintendent, a well-meaning neighbor who had a motive. In sympathy with my parents, he hoped to see me distinguish myself at work in a way I hadn't in college.

Suddenly city-bound, headed for Fort Dodge, population at least forty-thousand, I imagined myself as Lois Lane storming Gotham, fully anticipating a Clark Kent fling.

"By the way," Walt had said, lobbing a final question as an afterthought when I reported in for the first day of wage-earning work. "You can type, can't you?"

An image of the hallway outside high school typing class popped into my head like a rerun from a B-movie. To taunt me, a gang of boys would scoop me into the air and plop me like a potted plant into an oversized waste-basket outside the classroom door. Stuck, I stayed in the waste basket until a merciful janitor would come by pushing a broom and pluck me out or tip the basket on its side so I could crawl out. It was the boys' way of flirting and I loved the tease, but stranded in the basket, I missed skill-building exercises and had not learned to type.

"Oh, sure, I can type," I told Walt, hoping a speed of seventeen words per minute would help me outrun my past.

Walt assigned me to obits. I hammered keys like a crazy lady, hacking out *(&&&$@)#*()# until skill and accuracy built. Speed escalated to ninety words per minute and, in the interim, I turned on the charm. I smiled and sounded good, clacking the keyboard frantically when Walt walked by.

"You need to tell me," Walt said. "I need to know."

He wanted details.

"I walked over to the Country Kitchen," I told him in Catholic-school mode, as if in a confessional. If I had to tell, I decided to tell it all and suffer the penance. "I went by myself because I was upset. Jay had really been bothering me."

It was the custom for reporters to break for lunch after putting the first edition to bed, about one-thirty every afternoon. As a group, we would meander down the sidewalk, pick a high-backed booth in a cafe that ran paid ads in *The Messenger,* and fill an hour with gossip-level commiseration before heading back to the news-room for -30- calls. Stories were swapped over lunch and, most days, Jay fantasized that high-circulation papers like the *Cedar Rapids Gazette* would be grateful to have a Farm Editor, a Texas Aggie, of his caliber. They would pay him what he was worth. He supposed he would ap-ply. I wished he would. I had tired of Jay's remarks and personal complaints, his voluble and constant charge that *his wife wouldn't give him any,* that she cared only about the three kids he called rug rats.

"Maybe you need to be nicer to her," I offered once at lunch, defending a woman I had never met. His com-plaints, I thought, were private matters of marriage and his callousness, an officious disguise. He made me think of a whistle or some other small, shrill thing that issues a sharp, irritating sound.

"Like a queen," he said. He flattened his back against the upholstery, chest out, arm tossed over the booth's top border, stretching self-satisfactorily. "I treat the woman like a queen. That's what she thinks she is."

Jay's eyes ricocheted when he talked. His laugh erupted in snorts, his face contorting like a carved horse head on a merry-go-round with exaggerated lips baring matchstick teeth in an unreal effect. Slick with Vitalis, his hair pointed like coated feathers and left a greasy odor in his wake. He might have been forty—old, I thought. To work, Jay wore the requisite white shirt and striped tie, khaki pants; on assignments, he walked bean fields with a navy blazer slung over one shoulder as if he were a politician shooting a campaign ad. He ran pictures of himself strolling fields and country lanes with farmers in overalls, measuring crop growth or assessing hail damage. He spoke to farmers empathetically; but he spoke of women as if they were worthless tokens he used to fill holes in his pockets.

Potential paramours for Jay to target in the newsroom numbered only three, though each was unmarried since wives and mothers had not penetrated the work force. Dorothy, Regional Editor, a maiden who had snuffed forty-four candles on her birthday cake, secured her modesty by wearing long-sleeved, high-collared white blouses bound at the neck with a pert bow. Gross grain ribbons held hair that Dorothy continued to braid like a junior high girl long after her tresses had turned gray. She shared her parents' home and accompanied them to Friday night church suppers because a girl needs to have a little fun, she explained in a nasal, unmodulated voice. Barbara edited society and was by nature, social. The parade of men she entertained in her downtown apartment inspired guys in the composing room to name her the Office Punch Board. Childless and divorced, Barbara dressed as if in uniform: a lace-collared suit in navy worn with matching two-inch pumps. Her hair, a page boy in a shade of henna, puffed into an unnatural fullness and refused to move in the wind. I believed she wore a wig and I tried not to stare, though I wondered if she took it off at night and laid it on the night stand. I pictured her men friends hiding their surprise when seeing a bare-headed Barbara in bed. She had come from Minneapolis and, at age fifty, a small daily was the sled she rode on the down slope of her career, even I recognized that. The newsroom's girl trio was completed by me, a stereotype, the doe-eyed ingenue whose blonde hairdo had been shaped and sprayed into a flip. I liked the other two women, though they were what I promised myself I would never become, an old maid or a divorcee. I would marry and stay married, for sure.

The day I belted Jay, I yanked my purse out of the bottom desk drawer and crashed into the metal waste-basket next to my desk, almost falling, as I left the news-room before deadline. Angered by him, I had cut through noon traffic on Felix Street and comforted myself with the Big Burger Special and a glass of cold milk at Country Kitchen.

"I felt better after lunch," I told Walt. I had sorted through my anger, glanced at the clock, laid two wrinkled dollars on the table to cover the check and tip, slipped my arms into my coat sleeves, and walked back to work. I felt calm and rational when I walked up the stairs to the newsroom.

"So what happened?" Walt asked, scribbling on the open notepad, assigning an importance to my story, making it seem newsworthy.

"I wish I didn't have to talk about it," I said.

"Well, you do."

Outside Walt's office, Jay sat at his desk, typing farm reports, swimming in insouciance as if he were innocent. I tensed again, feeling him behind my back, the sense of his leer a constant. I cringed at his innuendoes, at his stealthy touch and his comments that had grown increasingly coarse. That morning, he had cornered me in a back room as I searched the morgue, a bank of file cabinets stuffed with categorized news clips, history. No one was near except two proofreaders who hunched over galleys, zealots dedicated to the cause of exposing typos and rooting out shameful errors before they appeared in print.

"I like your shirt," Jay had said.

My stomach muscles stiffened in a band across my groin as if I needed to wretch. I shielded myself with the metal barrier of a file drawer opened between us. I had sifted through files in search of clips featuring the local music scene, concert reviews of tour groups that had come through town—St. Louis Symphony, Kingston

Trio, and Country Western headliners at the Fort Dodge Barn Dance on Saturday night TV. Walt had asked me to localize a story on Beatlemania; I had moved beyond obits and had worked up to features. On top of the file cabinets, I had laid a wire story and photo showing the Beatles deplaning at Kennedy after flying in from Heathrow.

"It looks like silk," Jay said. He leaned into the open drawer and fingered the files.

Yes, the blouse was silk, a brilliant, pearl-buttoned blue. A cluster of blue jewels I had pinned to the shoulder tricked the light and registered as a complex of purple and green. The silk felt slick and cold on my skin though my face felt hot. I inhaled, head held down like a snorting bull, teeth clenched in a tight jaw. Jay had developed a habit of running his hand up my spine as he zipped by my desk. I hated looking at him, hated knowing he was near.

"It makes me want to rub your body all over," he said.

"I don't think so, Jay!" I slammed the drawer shut, hoping to snap his hand. I scooped up my Beatles picture—Paul, cute as a bug and Ringo looking vacant. I maneuvered my way past Jay, making sure not to touch him. I huffed out the door, my Irish dander up. Unable to concentrate, I rustled papers on my desk and visually mapped Jay's route as he slinked out of the morgue. His skinny arms dangled like a primate's and he crossed the newsroom, coming my direction, his face painted with a smirk. He rounded the corner of my desk. From behind, I felt his hand press my back near the waist and slide up my spine. His lean fingers veered and slipped under my arm, extending around my body, glancing, zipping across my right breast as he slinked by. His fingers were mercury, making my temperature rise fast as his hand. I felt my face burn; I burned all over.

That's when I left the newsroom. An hour later, I returned after thinking things through. I had decided to use reason, to confront Jay and tell him honestly how I felt.

His desk was the first inside the door. Reporters pecked at typewriter keys. Everyone was on deadline.

"Jay," I said. My voice halted his typing.

He stared up at me and, spring-loaded by instinct, my hand flew. I caught him on the left cheek with a fast right and he dropped to the floor. My aim was reckless, but true. At one-hundred and ten pounds, I was Cassius Clay.

"I'm sorry," I told Walt. "He looked at me. I looked at him. And *whop*! I hit him. I didn't know I was going to do it. I...I was...I only planned to talk."

Walt frowned. I sighed.

I filled the silence with a scene in my head, imagining the moment I would have to confess, not to Walt, but to Dad, telling him I had been fired for brazenness. Farm Editors in rural newspapers were bigwigs. And I slugged one.

I felt anxious, as if obligated to say more.

"If I were out in public..." I continued, though Walt had closed his notebook. "If I were out in the street, I might have to put up with someone like Jay. But I don't have to when I come to work."

I stated my case with unadorned honesty, believing what I believed.

Walt stood. He was very tall.

He hooked both thumbs in his waistband and gave his pants a jerk, hiking up the brown leather belt that had settled below the curve of his belly.

"You're right," he said. He opened his office door and released me to the newsroom, a little swimmer in the sea.

Next, Jay occupied the hot seat. His face purpled as he and Walt talked. I worked on my Beatles feature, calling around to set up interviews, *it's a hard day's night*, skipping through my mind. I watched Jay and Walt peripherally. After awhile, Jay exited Walt's office and went to work at his desk. He didn't run his hand up my spine on the way. He didn't touch anyone. He didn't say a word or look my way. It was as if I had already vanished from the newsroom.

The next morning, Jay was absent, his desk had been cleared, and Walt announced a search for a new Farm Editor. In time, I left *The Messenger*, too, after a Walt-taught course in ethics, personal integrity, and fact-checking.

By then, childhood over, the colorful blush of the world had dimmed to black and white. Walter Cronkite reported for CBS news, weeknights at six. Johnny Carson played Carmac and divined answers before questions were asked on late night TV. The *Today Show* aired before breakfast in the morning and featured swarms of Negro men marching on Washington, the flashing eyes of Dr. King illuminating their dream. Day after day, stories poured over desks in the newsroom, evanescently, sheets of black ink on newsprint. Even crimson blood stains on Jackie Kennedy's pink Oleg Cassini washed across the newswire in shades of muted gray. Lyndon Johnson appeared on network TV—the red, white and blue of America's flag bleached in the background, its splendor turned to sepia by news film. The President mouthed a speech writer's words. His lips opened and closed like Charlie McCarthy's eyes deadened on his stiff, wooden face as troops mobilized and shipped off to war.

A Kiss is Just a Kiss

Rain rushed in before dawn to rinse the bark on trees and bathe the lawn until new shoots of grass smelled sweet and clean. The temperature was neither warm nor cold; the day, a transitional one in the gray hours between winter and the birth of spring. Nature that morning seemed trapped in ambivalence, like me. Why, I wondered, had I agreed to meet Artie, both of us then married with children. I had no reason to believe—though, I might have hoped—that he who had once been important to me could be important again.

Artie had telephoned weeks before, his voice a surprise; I had neither seen nor heard of him since high school when I was young, hopeful, and in love. If I had thought of him at all in the flood of passing years, he had appeared like a celebrity preserved on an album cover in my mind. There, his faded youth retained, he stayed forever lean and athletic, not fat-faced and aging. Why not leave it that way?

"I'm coming to Kansas City to sing in barbershop competition," he said when he called—how had he found me? "I'd like to get together with you while I'm in town."

I imagined a cast of *Music Man*, Artie joining a quartet of stripe-jacketed, bow-tied businessmen reprising *Lida Rose* for community theater, singing from the heart. How small-town and genuinely American could he be? Still, I had said yes; I would see him in real life, in real time, though I felt as if he had been amputated from my life, his memory, phantom. It would be wiser, I thought, to trick the mind, to remember the way we were—in a school corridor, the day he chose me over Mary Sorenson. He invited me (sort of) to the Sweetheart Dance, senior year.

"Hey!" he said, singling me out between Geography and World History. He planted a hand against the wall above my locker, caging me in with one arm. Viking-sized hands and wrist bones showed below the cuffs of his shirt; his arms were longer than his sleeves. He leaned close, head down, tall as a giraffe bending to nibble tree leaves.

I smelled spices on his breath. The clatter of voices in the halls and the clang of slammed lockers receded; I concentrated only on him.

"Hey!" I answered back, snapping my locker shut to hide his picture taped to the inside. The shot was my favorite: Artie in his jersey, number thirty-two, going in for a lay up, his arm snaking toward the hoop, rocky knuckles and vine-like fingers wrapped around a basketball. I pressed the back of my head against the locker and felt the cold steel seep through my hair as Artie's eyes glanced on and off my face, making me aware of the chin pimple I had squeezed until it glowed lantern red. Artie had trained his eyebrows to form an inverted V, framing a Nordic face. His brows arched in a flirt, raised like roof beams. Behind his eyes, I felt that something smoldered as if a hurt had been stoked deep inside. Shyness veiled his secrets and layered him in hidden meaning, making him hard to interpret, like a line of poetry. Artie was musical, scholarly and agile, though less athletic than his four brothers who broke records on the basketball court. In that way, he hadn't measured up.

"You got a date for the dance?" he asked. "For *sweet-*

hearts," he teased, playing with the syllables, playing with me.

"No..." I said. "Do you?"

"I do now."

The night of the dance, I arrived late for the game. Mrs. Sheakley, owner of the shop where I worked, forced me to stay until after eight, her witch's voice corroded from the Lucky Strikes she smoked in the privacy of un-opened crates in the basement stock room. She knew I had a date, yet she scheduled me until store closing to dress the window in lace hearts and red ribbons pinned to pink cardigans or zip-front robes. Friends honked their car horns at me, a living exhibit in the display window as they whizzed down Main Street, headed to the game to trounce Storm Lake before the dancing began.

I rushed in at half-time as the band, heavy with tu-bas, played Sousa from center court. We won. Artie scored. And I hovered in the post-game shadow of the gym, waiting for him to bolt out of the locker room. He would see me, I thought, looking cute in a plaid skirt I had bought at Sheakley's, twenty-percent off. Mrs. Sheakley took it out of my check.

Artie spotted me when he shot through the door, fresh from a shower, fresh from a victory. We toe-flipped our loafers onto the heap of boots and shoes left at the door, and Artie led me into the gym with one hand, my fingers limp in his, Astaire and Rogers, parting the streamers in a crepe-papered gym. My skirt was so tight, I took baby steps and slid in my socks on a talcum-powdered floor. An audience of dateless non-dancers and adult chaperones clustered in bleachers, sidelined while I soared, light as the atmosphere, Artie's choice on the dance floor. We swayed, we sailed, and by the end of the song, we were balloons untethered, carried by a love ballad's breeze.

Now my broken heart aches with every wave that breaks, Pat Boone crooned from a record on the turntable...*over love letters in the sand*. Artie mouthed the words in my ear. I felt his breath in my hair and, my breath suspended, I anticipated the big dip he saved for the end of the song. If asked, I could not have explained the way Artie made me feel when I burrowed into the thick of his neck to inhale his scent, a mingle of Old Spice, Brylcreem, and Clearasil. We whirled, stocking-footed, around the floor of a gymnasium that still reeked of sweat from the game.

Afterwards, Artie cranked the heater to full blast and cracked the car window so carbon monoxide wouldn't poison us while we parked at Pike's Peak in fourteen-degree-below-zero. Tree branches were black etchings on a sky of midnight blue; the lake, a frigid white. We lodged in the car along the shoreline, implanted in snow up to the hubcaps and, in my mind, silver balls and pastel streamers still shimmered as we bedded down on vinyl upholstery in Artie's Pontiac, our bodies braided, moonlight piercing a layer of frost on car windows until we surfaced and I worried how long we had been there.

Minutes, I thought. Though it may have been hours.

Artie squinted and wiped lipstick from his face with his shirt sleeve. I ran my hands over myself, smoothing rumpled clothing, fastening things, fingering matted hair before heading home to sneak in without waking Dad. I clerked at the store the next morning, clocking in for Sheakley's Annual Sweetheart Sale with Mrs. Sheakley's satisfied cackle accompanying the cash register rings. Ginger stopped by to try on a Bobbie Brooks skirt and sweater set so we could swap stories in the fitting room and Mrs.

Sheakley would mistake Ginger for a paying customer.

"Did he say it?" Ginger asked, begging.

The words *I love you* from a date, especially a date with Artie, validated. Three words were sufficient to document a conquest since no one we knew had gone all the way, had actually *done* it, except a girl in our class who lived on the outskirts of popularity. While Ginger was in the store, I prompted her to peek over a half-wall into the next fitting room where Mrs. Pritchard, a be-back, a customer who couldn't make a decision without asking her husband, tried on Nelly Don dresses. I wanted Ginger to see hairs sprouting on Mrs. Pritchard's chest, a sight so freakish it stole my breath the first time I saw it.

"Yes..." I lied. I touched my fingers to my lips to remind Ginger to whisper. "He *said* it," I lied a second time. "But it kinda slipped out. I don't know if he meant it."

That was the trouble with Artie. He said nothing. Not a word about love. Or a picket-fenced future. When he went to Luther College, he left me for a church school where Catholic girls, even those who were hardly Catholic anymore, were unwelcome. He didn't call. He sailed off in the way he had loped down the center court, purpose-

207

fully. Without a word.

"If I live through this, I'll live through anything," I told Cookie, entrusting her with my sorrow once Artie was gone. If there had been anything I had feared losing, it was him.

He must have thought me to be a lesser star in his collection, as Pete had been in mine. I felt that fate, the gods, punished me not for deceit, but for shallowness. Pete had known all along that I set my sights on Artie and, given a chance, it was Artie I would choose. Like Pete, I wanted that which was beyond an easy reach, as if I had picked out a Christmas gift and sensed that it was unattainable or, worse, undeserved. In my small world, I understood the heart's cravings no better than I understood the wonders of the universe. Explained over and over again, love's mysteries made no sense to me.

Thankful once more to have Cookie as a companion, I lifted her from her snooze on a throw rug and squeezed her around the middle, snuggling with her on the bedspread's chenille welts, Cookie's heart beating like a bunny's, my heart feeling like it might crack. Cookie whined; I whined, too. Together, we whimpered under the clutter of a bulletin board nailed to the wall above the bed. There I had posted the remnants of high school: playbills, newspaper clippings, snapshots, odes written by my hand, dead carnations from a wrist corsage, a black and gold *E*, the varsity letter Artie had given me, and a wad of his already-chewed bubble gum, the taste of him still on it. Cookie sniffed the bedding, then chose my face as the focus of her attention. She spread herself flat as a toupee on my chest, pinned my shoulders with small paws, and smothered my mouth with her humid breath and wet nose, as if she understood. Artie was gone and I had not seen him since.

Then he called. Wanting to see me. Led by a blend of curiosity and courtesy in deference to old times—or was it vanity?—I dressed like a valentine when I went to claim the ticket Artie had reserved in my name, my married name, at the Music Hall box office. I slid my hips into my favorite Liz Claiborne, a red poplin skirt with a saddle-stitched jacket shaped at the waist. To hide a matronly crepe, I chose a long-sleeved, turtleneck sweater. Uncertain of my intentions (or Artie's), I drove downtown alone, leaving the man I had married puttering around home in his basement workshop, arranging fishing lures in a tackle box, his attention turned to Trout. My absence for the length of the afternoon would go unnoticed by him, a husband who had settled into a state that was not happy, not sad, not often sober.

Windshield wipers matched the pulse of the rain that had lingered beyond morning. I pulled into a downtown garage, underground, in a row near the entrance. I filed the parking stub in my purse and locked the driver's side door of my Mercury, an '86 two-door I had bought with my own income, a journalist's paycheck. I walked up the ramp and emerged in rain, soft as sea spray. Poised at the edge of the curb while traffic cleared, I listened to the hum of car tires swishing on wet pavement. I had won the Best Legs contest in college and, knowing my calves still looked sculpted in black hose and pumps, I ventured into Twelfth Street and crossed the road like a madame, stepping over puddles in shiny new shoes. That was what I wanted Artie to see, not a love-struck girl he had left in the past, not a middle-aged matron he surely expected, but a seasoned, shapely-legged woman who had lost all thoughts of him. Our reunion, I decided, was not to *see* him but to *show* him.

Inside the Music Hall, I settled into the velvet cushion of a theater seat, one over from the aisle, fourth row from the front. I crossed my legs and as my skirt drew up, exposing thighs, I caught the man next to me steal a glance. Thankful for the reassurance, I wondered what Artie would notice. House lights flicked and dimmed. The show opened and an exuberance that surpassed the leadenness I had anticipated surprised me. I felt captivated, unexpectedly engaged. On stage with the Cedar Rapids chorus, Artie looked mythological. His mess of curls threw patches of light. He was taller than ninety other singers, each dressed in a tuxedo, each courting me with an explosion of harmony, at first soft, then in vibrant, loving tones of *Once in a Lifetime.* As soon as he had performed, Artie joined the audience, slipping in beside me in the aisle seat he had saved for himself. His teeth shined white when he smiled in the half-tint of the auditorium. A waft of *Polo*, his choice of cologne upgraded since high school, made me inhale. Before I left home, I had misted my neck with *Décolleté*, an import from a shop in Brookside. I wondered if he smelled me, too. In the shadows, the legs of his tuxedo pants bulged with an athlete's firm quads and reflected the muted light in the way a satin ribbon would. His hair shimmered, white-blonde, not gray. His shirt laid flat against his chest under a row of pearlized buttons. His face had fleshed out, but if his waistline had thickened, a cummerbund concealed it.

"We're gonna win this thing," he whispered. His breath tickled. He lifted my fingers and squeezed my hand in his. I felt an inner vibration, as if one of the songs had strummed. It was nice to feel him next to me, breathing quietly.

"Let's get out of here," he said when the show closed. With one hand, he led me through the lobby, zigzagging between marble columns and crowds of patrons waiting for cabs inside the auditorium, out of the drizzle.

We walked directionless in the slow rain, ignoring it as we wound through the canyons of city sidewalks. Rainwater had trickled down cement and steel tiers as if buildings were rocky cliffs. Streams formed in the gullies. Workers had fled for the weekend, scooting away to suburban shopping malls or neighborhoods built on cul de sacs. Tourists had been lured into stores and restaurants, absorbed by the city. We were isolated, alone in city streets, sharing the intimacy of a soft, small moment, pure as a drop of rain.

We meandered, unbothered by anyone, rain misting our skin. At first, we both talked at once, stumbling conversationally, stepping on each other's words, fumbling for rules because there weren't any. I began to realize that what I felt in his company was neither uncertainty nor ambivalence. It was comfort; it was his muted charm. In no hurry, we strolled, circling several blocks on foot. We passed the Hotel Savoy, and I pointed at delicate veins on the Tiffany-glass face the hotel bared to travelers along Central Street. Down the block, we peered through plate glass into the darkened cavern of Kansas City's piano man, Tim Whitmer's place on the corner of Tenth and Central. Then we ducked into the cold, marble foyers of the Lyric and the Folly and, for Artie, I recounted each theater's history: each had claimed her stake in a cattle town's heritage, each owned her own legend, each had stood a proud matriarch on a city block, like two cold-shouldered sisters estranged by differences in lifestyles.

The Lyric's snooty venue catered to opera buffs, the socially elite. The Folly was born in untamed times of the wild west, then blossomed into burlesque. Though they had begun at the same time and place, their histories had divided them, as had ours, Artie's and mine.

By five o'clock, we had walked until our shoes were soaked.

"Let's go get a drink," he said. "Come on. *I* know a place. My hotel."

The implication sent a surge of anticipation through me; buried feelings flared in the mist of the afternoon. He took my arm and led me between tall buildings, around the corner to the Vista where a doorman ushered us through beveled-glass, double walnut doors dressed with brass handles. We flicked beads of water, tiny as sequins, from our shoulders and trailed through an art-lined corridor, the thick mosaic patterns of carpet absorbing our steps. Beyond the gift shop laid a grand foyer and the Walnut Room. A brass easel held a poster touting *Ida McBeth. Appearing Nightly.* We followed the host into a lounge that at that hour was as deserted as the rain-soaked streets. We took a marble-topped table for two; a fresh rose bloomed in a bud vase; a candle flickered in a smoked-glass vigil. Blue velvet chairs nested against a walnut pillar and we were hidden in its mass, as if it were a tree. Windows stood floor-to-ceiling; their stained wood framing a view of Barney Allis Plaza. Two spiny pine trees swayed as if there was music outside the window while jet-streams shot from the park's fountain, dancing, frolicking and cascading into a pool, outdoing the rain.

It was late afternoon, too early for the lounge to have filled for the evening. Two men drank at the bar. Otherwise, the room was ours, except for a bartender who wiped glasses with a cloth and a bow-tied waiter whose black garter pinched his shirt sleeve. A tuxedoed man took a seat on a corner stage, positioned himself on the piano bench, placed his fingers on the keys and his foot on the pedals beneath the baby grand, and played, the piano lid lifted like a wing above harp-shaped strings. The room filled with muted sounds of ivory keys tinkling. The clink of crystal touching crystal at the bar. The shift of a log in a lit fireplace. And a petulant rhythm of rain swishing against the window as if in a melancholy mood, making a sound like a brushstroke on the skin of a drum.

"Maybe I should call you Art. Since we're not kids anymore," I said.

"People do," he said. "Ar-*thur*. Coach."

"What can I bring you?" the waiter with the bow-tie asked. He set two napkins, white with a gold logo, on the table.

"Champagne," Artie said. "We're celebrating."

Cedar Rapids had captured the second place trophy and Artie was satisfied, though first-place was in their future, he claimed, competitive as ever. He liked to win.

He had brought pictures, wallet-sized snapshots of two kids and a woman named Kay, wife number two. She was pretty, smaller than me, and younger. She looked younger than him. I wondered how her life compared to mine. And I wondered what he had told himself about me, though what difference would his answer make? I decided on reticence; I wanted him to lead, to tip his hand, not see mine.

I sipped my champagne, feeling the bubbles stimulate my tongue. He drank his in gulps as if it were a bottle of beer.

We exchanged news, a synopsis of our lives, though

216

the superficial telling of tales rendered us ordinary, I thought. Two married people from two separate worlds, swapping stories of college-age kids, as if our children had made us instead of our making them, as if we did not exist as individuals, as if the evolution from what we were to what we had become had happened only by way of parenthood. Why at that moment, while looking at Artie's snapshots, did I remember an exchange between my sister and me on the eve of her second marriage, her first husband having died young? The scene between two sisters unrolled in my mind as if on a reel of home movies, uneven and flickering. The sun had shined on us two sisters that afternoon; Barb and I had warmed to it, she—a bride-to-be—relaxing in an easy chair; I cozying into a Bentwood rocker.

"I've never been loved by a man," I confessed for the first time, my sister as witness, the night before her wedding. "Not in the way you think a man loves a woman."

She looked at me, a sadness changing the shape of her eyes.

"I'm sorry," she said and I knew she meant it. "I can truly say I have been loved, really loved, by at least two men."

Why not me, I wondered.

Why hadn't Artie loved me enough to keep me? Or did he wish he had? I wanted him to tell me, to bridge the years, but I did not ask because, in truth, I was afraid to know, afraid to unveil the pain of my own inadequacy, my failure as a lover, a woman unloved. Why had he left so suddenly and what had driven him to see me now? Was it boredom, curiosity, or yearning? Questions swirled, though I realized that old truths did not need to be uncovered. I didn't want his life. I didn't want to be his wife. I had not longed for Artie. My longing was for love.

I looked at him again and I felt my senses bubble from the champagne and from his company, my husband at home, Artie's wife asleep upstairs in their hotel room. She had shopped in the afternoon, then napped. Besides, Artie told me, she thought we would have catching up to do. I wondered if by withdrawing she demonstrated graciousness or indifference?

"How long have you been married?" he asked.

"A really long time."

Instantly, I regretted my answer. Had I shown a distaste for my marriage while he had revealed nothing? Except that he had a first wife and then, a second.

"Are you happy?" He surprised me with the directness of his question.

"I don't know." I shrugged.

I had lost touch with the concept of happiness in a life I had learned to choreograph as a round of dutiful steps.

"Attorneys don't have wives," I said. "Attorneys have domestics. Someone who's on call. Someone to make them look good. Appear successful."

Why did I show my embittered, obsequious self? Had I grimaced unattractively when I spoke? Still outmatched by Artie's gamesmanship, I felt I had fouled as he finessed.

"Are you?" I tossed the question back.

"I don't know." He shrugged, as I had. "I should be. Kay's nice. I've got a little money put away. Have a winning record. Most the time."

I sipped from the glass, returning my mouth to the stain on the rim where I had already left a lipstick print. I resisted a temptation to touch his face with the sensitive part of my fingertips, to fondle the pearl, tuxedo buttons that descended in a line down the front of his pleated shirt.

I studied his features in light so dim there were no shadows. I searched his eyes. For what? A sign of regret? Did I need him to say he might have married me? And would we both then be happy?

"What more do you want?" I asked.

"I don't know," he said. "Do you ever feel like something's missing?"

I rimmed my champagne glass with the tip of one finger. He used his fingers to flatten the edges of the napkin he had folded into a shape like a boy making airplanes out of paper, our body language taking the place of words. I realized that we flirted with feelings that had not disappeared, but had lurked in the years.

"Are you still a good dancer?" I asked.

He stood.

"C'mere," he said, looking down on me with his half-smile, leading me to a small square that was the dance floor near the piano.

"How about *As Time Goes By*?" Artie asked and the piano player played.

On tiptoes, I stretched to wrap my arms around his neck. The stubble on his face, short, sharp hairs from the day's growth, stimulated my cheek and, as we danced, I ran the flat of my palm along the gabardine on the back of his tuxedo, smoothing the roughness of his jacket and, beneath it, stroking the bone-hard ridge of his shoulders, wide as a horizon. He placed his hands at the small of my back and pressed. A line from Yeats drifted on the music in my mind and I wondered, *How can we know the dancer from the dance?*

I stopped and stood perfectly still as Artie kissed me, not hard, soft. He tasted sweet, like pastry. I examined his face, his skin, fair and light. His lips, plump as they were long ago when he had pressed them against his trombone. I touched a crease at the corner of his eye and followed it like a path. Afraid to loose a flood of feelings, I made a cuff with my fingers and clasped his wrist, raised his arm, and turned his watch, face up.

"It's seven," I said. "Your wife will be awake."

He nodded.

"Yeah," he said. "I told her we'd go out tonight. Do the town."

I asked Artie not to walk me to my car. He had left me standing once. Not again. I took the lead, walking him to the elevator, like a hostess escorting a guest to the door, exchanging pleasantries, the party over.

He pressed the up button. The bell pinged.

"This was nice," I said to the man who was as he had always been, one I loved to kiss. Nothing more needed to be said, only imagined with the details of our lives left unasked and unanswered, lost in ambiguity, as if the afternoon had been lifted out of context like a sentence in a story that had a beginning, a middle, and no end. He stepped inside the elevator, turned his back to the wall, and I watched the doors slide across his face. He had come and he had gone, a glint of gold, encased in time's clouded dome.

I left the Vista. Lit by street lamps and scattered stars, the nightscape glowed. Rain had stopped but droplets lingered on the hem of the hotel awning as if reluctant to fall into a pattern of beads that puddled on the sidewalk beneath tbe point of my toe. Leaves and twigs had been pitched, scattered and strewn on the avenue. Pansies in a window box, half-flattened in their soil, had again raised their rain-fresh faces, ruffled and unsettled, though un-damaged by the storm.

I drove the prudent route, home to my husband. I found him holed up in his basement workshop. He didn't ask where I had been or why. I felt heartbreak in his in-difference. Yet I, residually Catholic, confused by fear and duty, determination and disappointment, ached from a sliver of hope, not knowing that our union had streamed into treacherous waters.

"You know, it's not too late for us," I said. "We have the balance of our lives."

"We'll see," he answered.

It was natural to look back and wonder how and why as a couple we had let ourselves be swept over the falls. I had loved him once—had he never, like Artie, loved me? It seemed not long before that he had driven home with me to meet Mom and Dad at a barbecue in the backyard. After dark, the charcoal burned down beneath grates of the grill and on a bed of grass near Dad's putting green, I succumbed. In a single, sensual act, the night unfolded in a way that would make one summer last a lifetime. Under the weeping willow tree, he slipped over and in me as if he were hot liquid. The moon was a communion wafer in the sky, pure, white and radiant. Across the yard, light in the kitchen window cast a cold, glaring stare through a veil of tree leaves. I closed my eyes and pushed off for unknown shores with the man I would marry, the man who would father my sons, the man I would try to murder by hacking him to death with the spike of a high-heeled shoe.

five island diaries: stories of love, lost and found

First Island: Close to Shore
Post-World War II to Vietnam
Spartan Press May 2007

forthcoming
Second Island: Deep Waters
Martin Luther King to Man on the Moon

Third Island: Loosed Boats Floating
Liberation Armies to Love Canal

Fourth Island: Splash
Mega-moguls to MTV

Fifth Island: Brave New World
A Century Ends on Manhattan Island